## "I know your type," she said scornfully

"And just what type is that?" Barrett asked. His voice was casual, but his eyes were wary and waiting.

"You're the type who can't enjoy the simple life," Sherri accused. "I know. I was married to a man like you. He thrived on danger. He's dead because he couldn't enjoy the everyday pleasures. A calm, peaceful life with me just wasn't enough. The two of you were cut from the same cloth!"

"How dare you," Barrett snapped.

"I dare, because I know. He lived his life as one great adventure. Better to die gloriously than live a dull life, that was his motto. Just like you, Barrett. So you keep your kisses to yourself, because I've buried one man like you already and I have no intention of doing it again!"

**Anne Marie Duquette** has traveled extensively throughout the United States, first as an air force "brat" and then as a member of the military herself. She started her writing career as a young girl, with lengthy letters to relatives and friends describing her impressions of countless new duty locations. Now married to a naval petty officer and the mother of two young children, she continues to travel, but considers the Rocky Mountains her real "home." *An Unlikely Combination* is her first Romance—but readers will be pleased to know it's not her last.

# An Unlikely Combination

**Anne Marie Duquette**

# Harlequin Books

TORONTO • NEW YORK • LONDON
AMSTERDAM • PARIS • SYDNEY • HAMBURG
STOCKHOLM • ATHENS • TOKYO • MILAN

ISBN 0-373-02918-7

Harlequin Romance first edition July 1988

Dedicated to
Roger
&
Adrienne

# CHAPTER ONE

"LOOK AT ALL THESE COMPLAINTS! Just look at them!"

Sherri Landers flinched at the thud of her personnel file hitting her supervisor's desk. She stood at attention, her posture as stiff as the starch in her forest ranger's uniform.

"They're about you, Miss Landers," Robert Holden informed her. "Every single one of them. All these complaints are from the various partners who've been assigned to you. Shall I acquaint you with the contents?" he inquired in a voice that grew increasingly louder.

"That won't be neces—" Sherri started to say.

"Be quiet!" The gruff command was barked out, and Sherri jumped. The chief of the Rocky Mountain Park ranger staff settled his large bulk more comfortably into his chair.

"Now let's see. Where to start, where to start?" He flipped through the stack, muttering sarcastically, "There's certainly enough to choose from. Ah, here's a good one."

"'Miss Landers refuses to take suggestions from her partners and frequently ignores orders from ranking rangers,'" Holden read.

"I know who wrote that," Sherri broke in. "It was after a rescue, and he was just annoyed that I ended up making the right decision and he didn't," Sherri said, defending herself. Her gray eyes flashed as she remembered how the two children she had saved would have died if she'd listened to her higher-ranking partner.

"Did I ask for any comments?" came the deceptively soft voice of Robert Holden.

"No, sir," Sherri answered, trembling with indignation at being silenced.

"Then let me go on. Let's see here. 'Miss Landers is a loner...not part of the team...not open to others' advice...unwilling to obey orders if they don't agree with her plans...bad for morale....' You're also bad for my blood pressure, Miss Landers! I'm tired of reading complaints about you. If you weren't my best tracker, and if you weren't so infuriatingly right all the time, I'd have fired you ages ago!"

Holden illustrated his words with a slam of his meaty fist on the desk, and in spite of her outward composure, Sherri felt more than just a moment's worry. She had received lectures before on her behavior, but this time it was serious. Was she up for suspension? Nervously she checked the pinned-up braid of chocolate-brown hair in back, then adjusted her broad-brimmed hat.

"You've been with us for five years, Miss Landers. Your actual work, when you aren't antagonizing your numerous partners or getting them replaced, has been outstanding. I can think of at least nine instances where the people we rescued would have been merely 'bodies recovered' if it weren't for your expertise. Therefore, I'm not going to reprimand you," Holden said.

Sherri's relieved sigh was cut short as he continued.

"I have something better in mind." A slow smile spread across his ruddy face, and Sherri was instantly on guard. She knew her boss too well not to know that the particular smile he was wearing boded ill for her.

Holden tossed another brown file across the desk. "Pick it up, Miss Landers," he said, giving her a satisfied grin.

Sherri did and gasped as she read the name "M. S. Barrett," aloud. "Just what is this supposed to mean?" she asked with a sinking feeling.

"Exactly what you think it means. You're holding the file of the man who's been in a neck-and-neck race with you in making my job a misery. Why, he's alienated almost as many partners as you have."

Sherri knew what was coming, but still she pleaded for another solution. "You can't assign me to this man! He refuses to work with women!"

"That's right," Holden agreed. "He's gone through every woman I've assigned him. None has lasted more than a month. You're next on the list."

Here Sherri finally stood at ease, then leaned forward to brace her hands against the desk. "So assign him a man! Heaven knows he's requested one often enough. And then assign me a female partner."

"You know our policy, Sherri. Man-woman teams work out better in the field. There's much less working friction, and a woman's intuitiveness coupled with a man's greater physical strength makes for better success during rescues. And as the numbers of men and women are about equal here, I see no reason to change the rules for either one of you."

"But—"

"There are no 'buts' about it! You wouldn't be happy if I assigned you a saint as a co-worker. Maybe if you and Barrett take out your frustrations on each other instead of on me, I might just reach my retirement."

Robert Holden rose and looked straight into Sherri's eyes. "This time, Miss Landers, I'm laying down the law. You will work with Mr. Barrett. He will work with you. If the two of you are not successful partners, the State of Colorado will fire you, and not recommend either of you for further employment. Do I make myself clear?"

Sherri took a step backward, then gave him a tight nod. "May I leave now, sir?" she asked in a strangled voice.

"Not yet. Take his file, and acquaint yourself with your new partner. I've given Mr. Barrett yours, and I expect him to do the same. Tomorrow morning at seven sharp, I want you both here to be briefed on your new assignment. I'm sending the two of you out on a mapping survey. By the time you get back, you'll either be a good working team, or you'll be two people on your way to the unemployment lines. Good day, Miss Landers."

Sherri carelessly snatched up the file and stormed out of the room. As the door banged shut behind her, Robert Holden lit a cigar and puffed with contentment, muttering something about two troublemakers who were more than a match for each other.

Sherri hurried back to her cabin with long, angry strides. Her duties were done for the day, since she had started her shift well before dawn. She'd planned to spend the afternoon riding, but she was too upset for that now. Entering the small cabin she shared with another woman ranger, she threw her hat, the file and then herself onto her bed.

"I can't stand it!" she complained aloud. "I just cannot believe this."

A smaller woman poked her head around the bathroom door. "Hello, Sherri. Bad morning?" Janet VanHeusen was not used to stormy moods from her usually calm roommate. An outburst like this warranted attention, and Janet paused in the middle of getting ready for her own shift.

"Something like that," Sherri said, slightly ashamed of her behavior.

"Want to tell me what's wrong?" Janet asked, her voice quiet and soothing.

"I've been assigned a new partner. You'll never guess who it is." Sherri frowned at the memory.

"Barrett," Janet answered with conviction as she started to dress in a clean uniform.

"Yes, but how did you know?" Sherri wondered, unable to hide her surprise.

"Oh, Sherri, I've seen it coming for a long time. We all have," Janet replied, referring to her fellow workers.

"Then maybe you could explain it to me."

Janet hesitated. "Honestly?"

Sherri nodded. "Don't sugar-coat it, Janet. Whatever you have to say, I promise not to hold it against you."

Janet took a deep breath and began. "Sherri, I hate to be the person telling you this, but no one wants to work with either one of you on a day-to-day basis. Oh, you're both valuable in an emergency situation," she hastened to add. "Your knowledge of the terrain and your ability to follow a trail in the worst conditions is unsurpassed. And Barrett has to be either the bravest or the craziest ranger we have. He'll attempt any rescue, no matter how dangerous, and crack jokes while he's doing it. The two of you are valuable in a clinch, but beyond that, well, both of you are... difficult." Janet was being kind, but Sherri still winced at the truth of her words.

"We all saw this coming," Janet continued. "It was only a matter of time. Barrett can't stand not being in charge, while you have no patience with anyone not as skilled as you. Holden had to do something, and teaming you up is the obvious solution."

Janet finished dressing in her uniform, as Sherri started to peel hers off. She knew there was no point in denying her roommate's words.

"You have my permission to tell everyone on the next shift about my new partner," Sherri said in a wry voice. "Maybe it will liven up their dinner hour."

"You know I won't say anything," Janet said loyally.

Sherri shrugged. "Go ahead, it won't matter. It will be all over the park by tomorrow anyway. Holden is sending us out on a mapping expedition. Knowing him, we'll be gone for months."

"Surely not that long," Janet said, sympathetically.

Sherri smiled at the friendliness in her voice. "I've always wondered why you never asked for another roommate, Janet."

Janet peered into the mirror, which reflected the combination bedroom-living room behind her, as she put the finishing touches on her light makeup. "I see a side of you the others don't. I see how you worry when you're looking for lost hikers or climbers. I see how calm and comforting you are when you do find them. And I see how very upset you are when you don't. You may not be Miss Congeniality, but if I were ever in trouble and needed help, you'd be my first choice."

Janet paused, then added, "You'd better take Holden seriously this time, and try to get along with Barrett. If you don't, you're going to get fired for certain, and there isn't a person in this camp who'll say it wasn't deserved."

"Not even you, Janet?" Sherri asked sadly.

"Not even me." Janet shook her head, closing the door behind her as she left.

Sherri watched her leave. Then, determined not to give in to depression, she started to pull the pins from her hair and loosen the heavy braid. As she thought about the chore of washing her waist-length hair, she sighed. It took forever to dry, and during the winter she had to guard against catching a chill. She really should get it cut and permed. Twenty-five was too old for her simple hairstyle, and having to pin it up whenever she went on duty was a bother. But since there was no beautician anywhere near this remote station, she would just have to live with the inconvenience for now.

A shower helped calm her somewhat. She changed into jeans and an ivory-colored blouse and brought her hair dryer into the main room, choosing a seat near a sunny window. As she began the familiar routine of drying her hair, she reviewed all the facts she knew about Barrett.

She had never worked with him, but in a station as isolated as this, one soon learned to recognize all the other rangers by sight. Rocky Mountain had a staff of more than fifty, but Barrett stood out—and not only because of his reputation. He was tall and muscled, a solid bear of a man, yet pleasingly graceful in spite of his size. She remembered that he had brown hair, not the deep chocolate of hers, but the common brunette so often found in the Midwest. He was at home in the outdoors; Sherri knew that. She had seen him move with the same quietness and sureness of foot that she herself possessed. And like her, he wasn't one to waste much time with straggling co-workers.

She could see why Holden might have paired them. The fact that neither of them had much patience with the less competent rangers had made life difficult for their assigned partners. Sherri wished now that she'd worked with him even once, just to have some impression of what the man was like. She hated breaking in a new partner.

Still, a few things stuck in her mind. Whenever the really unpleasant jobs came up, such as digging firebreaks, Barrett was always willing to volunteer. Sherri had been around long enough to know who the shirkers and complainers were, and Barrett wasn't one of them. Not only that, she realized with a start, but he had almost as many successful rescues as she did, and she led the rest of the camp in that area.

Sherri shut off the dryer, even though her hair was still partially damp. She used a comb to straighten out the dark tangle, then decided to let the rest air-dry while she gave her attention to Barrett's file.

"M. S. Barrett," Sherri read aloud. "Hmm. I wonder what the M. S. stands for?" She couldn't remember the man being addressed by anything other than his surname. He was thirty-six, a former Marine who had served overseas for four years. After that came a list of jobs that made Sherri's head swim. Oil-rig worker, mountain guide, chef, ranch hand: the list seemed endless. The man was well educated, and successful at each new endeavor. He'd held dozens of jobs, but had been released from each one because of "personality conflicts," despite his "excellent work performance." He'd been working with the Rocky Mountain National Park System for three years now, the longest time at any job since the military. And he was still single. Not divorced, not widowed, but single. At his age, that made him a confirmed bachelor, Sherri thought.

She turned to the category of Personal Attributes, where she read, "Mr. Barrett is a hard-working individual who performs to perfection any job he undertakes. He works well with little supervision, is a quick learner and is entirely trustworthy." Not bad, Sherri thought. So why the varied work record?

"Mr. Barrett has a problem working with women, particularly in taking orders from them. In light of changing social standards, this attitude must be corrected if Mr. Barrett is to have any hope of future career advancement."

Sherri thoughtfully closed the file. Well, well. Mr. Barrett didn't like taking orders from women. And she had two more years in the forest service than he did, which made her the senior ranger. He wasn't going to like that one little bit. Not that she would pull rank on him. He could do whatever he wanted, go his own way, and she would go hers. As she always did. Her primary job was saving lives and all she ever wanted from her partners was to be allowed to do that job.

Sherri shifted on the bed and crossed her legs comfortably. Her thick hair was still slightly damp and she closed her eyes against the glare as she tipped her head back to get the full benefit of the sun's rays. Bending her arms behind her neck, she gathered up the glossy strands and fluffed them up and out, trying to hasten the drying process. A smile crossed her face as she remembered how her mother used to do the same with her own cocoa-colored hair. She, too, had shied away from scissors.

Sherri was startled by a forceful knock at the door. It had to be someone for Janet; she herself received few visitors. Unwilling to relinquish her comfortable position, she called, "Come in."

"I'm sorry to disturb you, Miss VanHeusen," the visitor said. "I was told Miss Landers was here. Could you tell her I'd like to see her?" The man glanced around the small cabin, then looked pointedly at the closed bathroom door.

"I know she just finished her shift. If she's cleaning up, would you mind if I wait?"

"Please have a seat," Sherri answered, taking in the appearance of the man across from her and knowing instantly who he was. She was a tall woman, but Barrett practically towered over her as she rose and gestured to a chair. She remembered that curling shock of brunette hair, but she found herself surprised by two of the greenest, most piercing eyes she'd ever seen. Those eyes, along with a square jaw, a chiseled nose and well-shaped lips, made Sherri wonder why such good looks were wasted on a man who continually antagonized his female partners.

"By the way, I—" Sherri started to introduce herself, but she never got the chance to finish.

"I can't believe I'm being stuck with the camp witch," Barrett complained loudly. "I know you're her roommate, but surely you must admit that even I don't deserve such a fate." He missed hearing Sherri's indrawn breath as he slapped the brown file he'd carried in with him.

"You should read this!" he exclaimed. "Talk about horror stories."

"Maybe I just will," Sherri agreed. "Please, do go on," She coolly prompted, accepting the file.

Barrett ran one large hand through his hair and didn't notice the warning signal in her flashing gray eyes. "What can I say? You're the poor fool who has to live with her, so I'm sure there's nothing in there you don't already know about. Working every day with an arrogant, insufferable, camp know-it-all is not my idea of a pleasant partnership."

Sherri returned to her seat near the window and quickly scanned the file, noting with relief that nothing of the sort was listed under her personality profile. She was described as an employee who worked best alone, and whose team efforts were dubious except under extreme conditions. Sherri could live with those truths.

Tossing the folder down, Sherri gave Barrett her coldest stare and felt the satisfaction of seeing him become a little disconcerted.

"Did it ever occur to you that Sherri and I might be good friends?" she asked quietly.

"No," he said, a trace of uneasiness evident in his voice. "Everyone around here knows she's got hardly any friends, male *or* female. I know she's kind of plain, but even if she wasn't, her personality would scare most people off. You ought to give her some beauty and character tips. She could use the help."

Sherri drew in a deep breath, angry at the insult. The dark-green unisex uniforms were far from flattering, and the same was true of her braided bun and the broad-brimmed hats they wore. She knew that none of the female rangers looked her best in uniform. However, in street clothes she was a tall, lean woman whose finely conditioned muscles couldn't hide her gentle, sloping curves. Her silver-gray eyes were dramatically set off by her straight dark hair, and the stubbornness of her chin was softened by lush, full lips that always looked somehow out of place under her all-business ranger hat.

And even if she were as plain as he thought, she resented being judged on her looks alone. Being a ranger was a tough job for anyone, and Sherri had worked hard to get this far with the ranger service. But what she resented most of all was his statement that she had few friends. She knew she wasn't popular. But that was her own problem, and she didn't need this man with his bad manners reminding her of it. And what right did Barrett have to criticize her, anyway? He wasn't exactly an outstanding social success either.

"Would you care to hear your own personnel rating?" she asked with silky softness.

Reaching for the end table beside her, she lifted his file out of the drawer into which she'd hurriedly thrust it. Then she carefully read aloud Barrett's personality assessment, ignoring his growing anger. On an impulse, she decided to ad-lib.

"Mr. Barrett lacks manners and tact, and is too deficient in the basic courtesies to ever advance in the working world. His intelligence is so limited that he does not even bother to ascertain the identity of the person in front of him." Here Barrett paled visibly as realization dawned.

"My conclusion is that Mr. Barrett should go ahead and resign, and save himself the disgrace of being shown up by Miss Landers." Eyes blazing, Sherri tossed his file contemptuously aside. "That's me, by the way. Now get out of my cabin."

Barrett stood up, his tall form menacing, but Sherri wasn't intimidated. "Here," she said, retrieving his file. "I think I've read—and seen—enough. And I promise you that I will do everything in my power to live up to any expectations you might have of me."

Then she stood up, her hair swinging and glistening with the movement, her face flushed with color. She strode to the door and jerked it open.

For a moment Barrett's face softened with what Sherri thought was regret. He looked...well...almost attractive without that habitual scowl of his.

"Please, please, don't beg my forgiveness," she said sarcastically. "I accept your well-mannered apology."

The insulting words brought that closed look back to his face. "Have it your way, partner." He emphasized the last word. "And I'll make sure I live up to all your expectations, too," he promised with narrowed eyes.

Sherri started to slam the door, then reined in her temper and closed it softly instead. She flopped down on the couch, her limbs shaking, and cursed herself for being a fool. Everyone knew the man was difficult. There was no need to make an active enemy of him before they'd even started their working relationship. And she could have sworn Barrett was about to apologize. Besides, much of what he'd said was true....

Sherri rested her chin on her hands, her long hair draped like a shawl around her shoulders. She hadn't always been so unfriendly, so difficult to get along with. Once, she was a pleasure to be around. Well, she'd have to make an extra effort to be cordial and cooperative with Barrett. Her job depended on her partnership with the man, and if anyone got fired, she was going to make certain it wasn't Sherri Landers.

The next morning arrived sooner than Sherri would have liked. At seven o'clock sharp, she entered Holden's office, observing that Barrett was already there, waiting. Holden soon joined them.

"Good morning, Mr. Barrett. Miss Landers. I trust you slept as well as I did last night." He chuckled to himself, obviously enjoying the baleful glares they were exchanging.

"I see you two have met." Holden reached for the files they'd returned, then motioned them to sit.

"Now, about your assignment," he began.

Fifteen minutes later, Sherri and Barrett were outside in the brisk morning air. Sherri shivered, for this was high country and mornings were cold, even in August. She decided to head for the canteen and get coffee and breakfast. By the sound of the footsteps behind her, Sherri knew that her new partner was following closely.

"Shall we have breakfast together?" he asked reluctantly.

"No, thank you. Remember me, the woman with hardly any friends? I'm used to eating alone."

"It doesn't matter what you're used to," Barrett replied nonchalantly. "We have a scant two weeks in which to survey hundreds of miles of mountainous country. We also have only one map, which I possess. In the interests of practicality, shouldn't we study it together?"

"I don't wish to," Sherri answered, ignoring the stares of curious onlookers as Barrett effortlessly kept up with her long strides.

Suddenly he grabbed her arm and whirled her around. "Listen here, Landers, I'm assuming you got the same ultimatum that I did. We work together, or we get fired together. For the sake of my job, you had better do yours."

Sherri looked disdainfully at the offending hand, then easily brushed it off. "Perhaps I should rephrase my answer. I don't *need* to look at the map. I could hike up there blindfolded."

Barrett stared at her in disbelief. "That's unexplored country! That's why we're being sent up there: to scout out new trails so the park can replace the ones ruined by the landslide this spring. You couldn't possibly do that without a map."

Sherri said nothing. Everyone knew of her reputation as the best tracker in the outpost. But no one knew that she had spent all her childhood summers up in the lonely mountains with a gold-obsessed father who explored every nook and cranny with a trained prospector's eye.

"Why don't you ask my roommate if you don't believe me? Just be sure you get the right person this time," Sherri warned.

She strolled ahead and entered the canteen. A few seconds later Barrett entered and stood beside her. Conversation gradually ceased as the morning diners noticed them, then everyone broke out in satisfied applause and cheered the new team. Barrett gave a sardonic bow, understanding their relief at no longer running the risk of having either Sherri or himself as partners. He wore a slight, mocking smile as he joined the chow line.

Sherri could not adopt his devil-may-care attitude. Biting her lower lip, she bowed her head and asked for "Just coffee, please," in hushed tones. When her order was ready, she walked quickly out the door. Barrett hurried to the window, and was just in time to see her leave the cup on the outside porch before heading back to her cabin.

Sherri reached her room without meeting anyone and was doubly grateful that Janet was working the morning shift. She flung down her hat, then turned on the hot plate and prepared to make some instant coffee. It wouldn't taste as good as the canteen's fresh brew, but anything was better than enduring the stares of all those people.

She started gathering up her gear in readiness for the next morning, which Holden had specified as their departure date. She rummaged through her drawers for clothing, glad at least that she wouldn't be required to wear the ranger's greens while on mapping duty.

The water was boiling heartily in a few minutes, and Sherri made herself an extra-strong cup of instant. She grimaced as she tasted it and added another spoonful of sugar. Thanks to her new partner, it looked as though breakfast was out of the question this morning. She'd try to be sure he wasn't around when she went to the canteen at lunchtime.

As Sherri absently packed her gear, she wondered how she'd ever ended up in such a sorry state. She'd been happy once, so very happy. She frowned, remembering just how little of her past was included in her personnel file.

There had been no mention of the fact that she was an only child whose mother, always sickly and frail, had died when

Sherri was ten years old. The report said nothing of her gold-obsessed prospector father, who dragged his little girl with him on wild-goose hunts for treasure whenever she wasn't in school—and sometimes when she was. Her education had been erratic; from the primary grades through high school, she'd attended a little one-room school house an hour's ride away. After her mother's death, her father hadn't balked at pulling her out of school for extended treks into the wilderness. If her co-workers could see some of the desolate places she had survived in while just a child, they would understand why she was adept at wilderness skills. She'd had no other choice at the time. It was a case of adapting or suffering great discomfort, or even death. Sherri's father had disappeared into the mountains for good when she graduated from school and left to find work. She hadn't heard from him since. She assumed he was still alive, but there was no way for her even to verify that.

After her mother's death, Sherri's childhood was unnaturally lonely, but to the young girl, it seemed normal. Life away from the mountains later opened her eyes to society, and she greeted the strange new world with open arms. When she met Thomas Landers at seventeen, she discovered that dreams could come true. He was much older than Sherri, a military career man who welcomed the strange combination of self-sufficiency and vulnerability in his new wife. Sherri thrived on the feeling of being loved and cherished, and except for the fact that Thomas wanted to wait a while before they had children, all seemed perfect.

Until his sudden death six years ago. Sherri's mouth went dry again at the memory. She still mourned the waste of his life. Her heart still ached with the knowledge that she would never carry his children, and it burned at the irony that she had finally learned to love, only to be left alone once more. Before Thomas Landers, she had thought solitude was normal; now she knew it was a curse. But with her husband gone, Sherri had lost her lifeline to society, and suddenly she didn't fit in.

After his death, Sherri decided to leave the city, and returned to live in her father's cabin until she was accepted for a post with the forest rangers. These weren't the usual park rangers whom tourists found manning information booths and gift shops. The unit was a crack team of people skilled in fire fighting, surveying, and four-season search and rescue. The work was lonely, isolated, and exactly suited to Sherri's needs. Her tracking skills quickly qualified her for duty at any of the remote outfits, and she had chosen her present station as the one closest to her childhood home.

She had hoped to make friends among the forest rangers, but unhappily, this turned out not to be the case. The women were intimidated by her confidence and skill, and were envious of her looks. In spite of her lack of glimmer and gloss, Sherri's vitality, together with her flawless features and cascading hair, were a combination that was hard to upstage.

The men soon found that outdoors, Sherri could match them stride for stride. Her endurance was exceptional, and her knowledge of the wilderness unmatchable. Unfortunately, because of her limited association with people, her tact was non-existent. Sherri simply stated what had to be done, then went ahead and did it. She never tried to explain the reasons for her actions and left her partners to either follow her or go their own way. Those who contradicted Sherri usually proved to be wrong, while those who followed did so grudgingly, thinking her an arrogant show-off. They could not know that as a child Sherri was told to obey or take the consequences. She had learned to follow her father's orders for her own protection, and expected the same response now when she herself gave a command. Her knowledge was supported by a genuine concern for others' safety, and she was surprised and hurt when people resented what were only good intentions on her part.

She withdrew even farther into herself, and her alienation after Thomas's death grew into cynicism toward society in general. Most people at the ranger station relied on Sherri when there was trouble and left her alone when there wasn't. Sherri had accepted that, but now she was worried. Barrett didn't seem like the kind of man to leave her in peace. Like her he wanted things done his way, but unlike her he created waves if they weren't. Sherri preferred to walk away, while Barrett had a bulldog reputation for trying to bend others to his will. He had left more than one female ranger in tears.

Sherri anxiously rubbed her forehead, resolving not to let the man get under her skin. She drank the last of her coffee and noted with satisfaction that she was almost finished packing. All that remained for her to do was ready the horses and tack and pick up food from the canteen. Sherri grimaced at the prospect of encountering her co-workers. At least she wouldn't have to face them after tomorrow. Suddenly she smiled to herself. The situation had to be pretty bad if two weeks in the wilds with Barrett was beginning to look good.

It was almost noon when Sherri heard a knock at the door. She put down the rations list she'd been working on, then crossed the room to see who it was.

"Hello. May I come in?" Barrett's words were polite, even if his tone held no warmth, and Sherri silently gestured him in.

"I see you're almost ready," he observed. Like Sherri, he had changed out of his ranger uniform and wore jeans with a flannel shirt, the sleeves rolled up as a concession to the fleeting warmth of the noon sun.

"I'm sure you didn't come to check if I packed according to regulation," Sherri said with some asperity. "What do you want?"

Barrett helped himself to a seat without waiting for permission. "I can assure you this isn't a social call," he said dryly, and Sherri simmered at the put-down. "I'm here to discuss plans for our trip tomorrow, if that's acceptable." He didn't wait for her to comment, but started right in.

"What time do you plan on leaving?"

"As early as possible. Probably an hour after dawn, or earlier if the mist is burned off by then," Sherri answered.

Barrett nodded. "That's fine with me. What about transportation?"

"I've already checked with the motor pool," Sherri told him. "I have a Land Rover reserved."

"A what?" Barrett frowned with displeasure. "A smaller Jeep would be easier to maneuver."

"True," Sherri agreed, pulling the hairpins from the bun at the back of her head. They were starting to irritate her scalp. "But I need the extra power to pull a horse trailer."

"What horse trailer?" Barrett demanded. His brows were pulled even lower in an unattractive scowl, and Sherri sighed.

"The trailer that is going to carry the horses we'll need," she explained with exaggerated patience. Her hair, now freed, fell heavily onto her shoulders, then bounced off and down her back. Sherri exhaled her relief, and began to braid the mass into a single loose plait behind her neck.

Barrett started to speak, but stopped as he watched her. "I didn't think there were women left who wore their hair long anymore," he said in a voice that sounded almost admiring. At Sherri's curious look, he shook his head and briskly continued with business.

"There is no way that horses could negotiate those mountains. We'll have to drive up as far as we can with the Jeep, then hike," he said with an air of finality.

"You won't be able to drive more than twenty miles," Sherri protested heatedly. "The Jeep would be as useless as the Land Rover. And I don't intend to walk hundreds of miles when I can ride."

Barrett snorted. "Even if you're right about the vehicle, there isn't a horse in this compound that could negotiate those rocks."

Sherri checked her watch again, hoping she could make it in time for lunch and still convince this obstinate man of the futility of his plans. "Look, I have my own horses. I always ride them on the job. They're native mustangs, used to the terrain. I trained the pair of them myself, and a child could ride them."

"I'm taking the Jeep," Barrett declared.

"Fine," Sherri snapped. "Then I'll take the Land Rover and the horse trailer. Now if you'll excuse me, I missed my breakfast, and I'd prefer not to miss my lunch."

She started for the door, but the superior bulk of M. S. Barrett blocked her way.

"Move it, mister," Sherri ordered, her eyes a steely gray.

"Not on your life, lady," Barrett flung back. "Have you forgotten Holden's warning? No teamwork, no job. If we leave tomorrow in two different vehicles, we might as well sign our pink slips ourselves."

"You're right." Sherri sighed in disgust. "For once," she amended.

"I have a proposition," Barrett said, his large frame still blocking the door. "We'll start off with the Land Rover and the horses. Then, once out of sight, we'll split up for, say, three days. Whoever has the most success is in charge of the expedition and gives the orders for the remainder of the trip. Agreed?"

A slow smile spread across Sherri's face. This was going to be like stealing candy from a baby. "Barrett, you've got yourself a deal."

She then brushed by him on her way to lunch, leaving Barrett to watch her retreating form, the one long braid swaying with the slight rocking motion of her hips. Barrett pursed his mouth in a silent whistle, then erased the gesture, unwilling for anyone to see that flicker of appreciation.

# CHAPTER TWO

THE NEXT MORNING'S SUNRISE was a spectacular blend of warm reds and oranges, but it was wasted on the station's new team. Both Sherri and Barrett were engrossed in their own thoughts as they loaded their gear into the Land Rover. Sherri carefully avoided getting too close to Barrett, keeping an invisible buffer around herself. The fact didn't escape Barrett's notice. Much to her dismay, he gave her a look of wry amusement, then continued with his work.

A few other rangers were already up, dressed for their early morning shifts. Noticing the activity around the Land Rover, one pair wandered over to watch.

"Hey, you lovebirds, don't forget your marshmallows and sticks for those romantic evenings!" one woman called out to Sherri as she winked at her own partner.

"Barrett, I wouldn't go out into the woods alone with Landers," the male half of the team threw in. "You might not get back in one piece."

The partners laughed at their cleverness, then Sherri heard the other woman say in a voice that was meant to carry, "Good riddance! They deserve each other."

Sherri bent her head, her throat tight with humiliation, even though outwardly she appeared as detached as Barrett. Despite herself, her hands shook as she tried to hitch the safety chains to the horse trailer. Barrett glanced her way and frowned.

Straightening his massive form, he began to walk slowly and with deadly purpose toward the merry pair. The woman quickly turned tail and hurried away. But the male ranger stood his ground as Barrett continued to advance, and defiantly he tried to stare back into Barrett's diamond-hard eyes. For a tense moment, Sherri shivered with fear for the smaller man until he, too, gave in, and returned to his duties.

Sherri relaxed her taut muscles. She had the strangest impression that Barrett had done that for her, not for himself. The couple's smirking certainly hadn't seemed to bother him. Sherri had almost made up her mind to thank him when a nasty glare from Barrett changed her mind. It was as if he'd read her thoughts and was daring her to say something about it. Sherri swallowed hard and went back to her task. With no other interruptions, the two of them soon managed to complete their loading, sign out and be on their way.

Barrett drove. She made no comments or suggestions regarding the route he was taking, and he asked her for none. Sherri smiled to herself as she watched the man behind the wheel. She would be leaving him soon enough, and on horseback she'd be able to make up any lost time.

"Are you finding something amusing about all this?" Barrett asked, breaking his earlier silence.

"Yes," Sherri answered.

After a few moments Barrett pressed, "Well?"

Sherri smiled even more widely, surprising Barrett with her loveliness. "It's a private joke," she said smugly, and Barrett made a sound of disgust.

"I'll bet," he said curtly. "Where do you want to stop for lunch?"

"Anywhere you want," Sherri answered, just as curtly.

When Barrett found a clearing along the rocky dirt path they had been traveling, she immediately went to check on the horses. The animals were clearly displeased at the rough ride they had endured, and Sherri decided that now was as good a time as any to take off.

"Hey, what are you doing?" Barrett demanded as she unloaded the horses.

"Leaving. Remember our deal? The horses and I have had enough of your driving." Sherri saddled one horse, then began strapping her pack gear onto the other.

"Aren't you going to have lunch?" Barrett was clearly surprised at her actions. "Come on, you and I both know we're going to spend tomorrow taking those horses back to the station and starting all over again with a small Jeep. You might as well lose on a full stomach."

Sherri exhaled sharply. "Where's the map?" she asked through gritted teeth.

Barrett pulled out the map, and she snatched it away from him. Pulling a pen from her pack, she circled a location. "That's where I'm headed. I'll wait for you there for twenty-four hours, then I'm gone. Where's the radio?" she asked, referring to the portable radio that would enable them to stay in touch with the ranger station at moderate distances.

"What do you need that for?" Barrett stood up, plainly refusing to unpack the radio.

"You're keeping the map, so I'm keeping the radio," Sherri informed him. "It'll be one less piece of equipment you'll have to carry when you catch up with me."

"That does it!" Barrett threw his sandwich down on the Land Rover's hood and purposefully strode toward her. The horses whinnied and shifted about, and only when Sherri threw him a look of scorn did Barrett realize what he was doing and temper his movements.

"Wouldn't you know I'd get partnered with a stupid Boy Scout," Sherri complained audibly as she calmed the horses. Then, throwing him another disdainful look, she rummaged in the back of the Land Rover until she found the radio. She detached the smaller walkie-talkie and handed it to him.

"Here. When you get hurt, don't forget to call me so I can come and rescue you, little boy."

Barrett carefully positioned the walkie-talkie on the vehicle's front seat before he responded to her gibe. "If anyone gets hurt, it's going to be you, little girl," he mimicked. "I've survived things in the military that would make you pass out just thinking about them." The clipped, precise words didn't disguise his fury. "It'll take more than a few rocks and a frigid ranger to do me in!"

"Fine," Sherri yelled, this time startling the horses herself. "Only we're not in the military. The terrain is our opposition. There's a difference, and I know it, even if you don't." She drew a deep breath. "You have the map and my location. One hint, not that a big, brave man like you would ever need it. If you keep heading northeast, as your driving seems to indicate, you'll come to a small stream. It's not on the map, and you'll be tempted to cross it with the Land Rover. Don't. There's soft mud under that slippery shale. You'll mire down or even tip over, although the water's not too high on account of the low snowfall last winter."

"Thank you, Davy Crockett." Barrett disregarded her words with a flick of his hand. "It's nice to be worried over."

Sherri tied the pack horse to her saddled mare and mounted. "I just don't want to have to rescue you," she said haughtily. "And I don't want anyone hurt—including you. That's my job, keeping people safe," she said, her voice serious now. "Remember what I said about that stream. Don't cross it. I'll be at that circled location for twenty-four hours after I get there, which should be around sundown. Check in on the radio then so I know you're all right."

Barrett laughed so hard he dropped the map. "You expect to make this much distance in one afternoon? What do you think you're riding, a flying horse?"

"Stay away from that stream," Sherri warned one last time. As she was riding away she turned and called back, "I packed you a second saddle in the horse trailer. Make sure you have it with you when you meet me. You're going to need it."

His gales of unbelieving laughter were the last sound in Sherri's ears as she left the area.

A few hours of riding helped calm her nerves. The smell of the pines, the dark jagged outline of the mountains against the clouds, and the rustling of wind in leaves wove an irresistible spell. Still, the beauty of her surroundings did nothing to lessen Sherri's uneasiness over leaving her partner alone. One of the rangers' cardinal rules was never to separate from your partner unless extreme conditions called for it. They all knew the buddy system was for everyone's protection. Barrett could easily be hurt in that treacherous shale stream or even killed if he fell into the shallow water unconscious from a blow to the head.

Sherri shifted guiltily. She had left him alone, and if anyone found out, she'd be fired for certain. The fact that he'd actually suggested their little wager was inconsequential. If he was hurt, she would never forgive herself. As for her own welfare, she wasn't worried. Not only were her horses in excellent shape, but she had plenty of supplies and the advantage of being familiar with the terrain. All Barrett had was a Land Rover and a map.

Landers, you idiot, she thought to herself. Now that she'd reached her destination, Sherri was growing steadily more anxious about Barrett's progress. Still, he had promised to check in by radio. If she didn't hear from him at sundown, she would go back after him. That resolution eased Sherri's mind somewhat, and she began to scout the area for a place to camp. She hadn't started climbing yet, so there were still a few clearings with grassy meadows that would be good for the horses. Sherri quickly decided that one location a ten-minute ride south would serve well as a camp.

She swung over, and was soon busy pitching her tent and gathering wood for a fire. She watered the horses, then picketed them in a lush grassy clearing. She was particularly careful to set up the radio where it would receive the maximum range. Then she settled down to wait.

The remaining hour or so until sunset seemed unbelievably long. Sherri tried to make contact with Barrett herself, but probably in the interests of saving the batteries, he hadn't switched on the walkie-talkie. She checked on the horses, spent longer than usual preparing a dinner and scouted the surroundings over and over again to pass the time. The last rays of the sun were disappearing and Sherri had just about decided to go back after Barrett, when the radio crackled in the stillness.

"This is mobile one, this is mobile one. Do you copy, base?"

Sherri ran to the radio with relief and grabbed the transmitter. "This is base, mobile one. We read you loud and clear. Over."

"Same here, base. Report?"

"No problems, mobile one. Your report?" There was a pause, and Sherri frowned.

After a moment Barrett said, "No problems, base. Everything is as boring as boring can be." There was another pause. "Are you still on the prearranged map coordinates?"

"Roger, mobile one, and I will be for twenty-four hours. Barrett, are you okay?" Sherri asked, dropping the formal transmission etiquette in her worry.

"Roger, base, Roger. Just checking. Over and out."

The radio static went dead at the other end, and Sherri cursed. He didn't sound okay at all. The idiot had probably flipped the truck; he was probably on foot—and might even be hurt! With that stupid pride of his, he was probably hiking his way here right now, refusing to admit he needed help. Damn!

"Base to mobile one, over?" Sherri played with the cord of the mike, then tried again. "Base to mobile one, over? Come on, Barrett, I know you're out there!"

He wasn't answering. Sherri checked the sky, still partly lit by the last of the setting sun, and made her decision. Racing into the tent, she grabbed some spare clothes, a first-aid kit and the strongest flashlight she had, then fastened them to her utility belt.

She was going to take only one horse, as it would be dark soon, and she didn't know how well Barrett could ride even in the daylight. Besides, if he were injured, they would have to ride double. Sherri didn't bother to saddle up, not wanting to waste a minute of the precious light. She had ridden Ladybug ever since the mare was a filly, and all she needed was her reins.

The mare was still full of energy and gladly took off at the fast pace Sherri set for her. Sherri rode quickly, expertly, one hand holding onto the reins, the other holding tight to the binoculars around her neck. They were infrared, and would help her even in the dark.

An hour passed, and Sherri was riding in shadow. Another hour passed, and now she was riding in blackness. The moon provided very little light. Sherri was beginning to doubt that she'd determined the correct coordinates for Barrett's position when she saw a flash of light to her left. Moving carefully to ensure Ladybug's footing, Sherri advanced toward the light.

It was Barrett, slowly making progress to her camp. His flashlight was pointed at the ground, and then at her as she approached. He saw a dark figure with floating brown hair on a strawberry roan horse. He'd never thought anything could look so good.

Sherri saw Barrett at the same instant, a wet, shivering figure in the darkness. He carried his backpack with his clothes and like the heavy, sodden sleeping bag on top, it was wringing wet. The spare pack that held his food was nowhere to be found. He was huffing and puffing like a steam engine and looked ready to drop. As Sherri passed her flashlight beam over him, she noticed one more thing. In his arms was the hand-tooled, dark leather saddle with the initials S. L. on the side.

Sherri smiled a slow, womanly smile. "Need a lift, stranger?" she offered in an inviting voice.

"If you're going my way," Barrett said calmly. "And if it isn't any trouble."

Sherri grinned to herself in the dark, feeling a sense of overwhelming relief, and slid down from the mare. He didn't sound like an injured man. Looping the reins around a tree branch, she took the saddle out of her partner's arms. Some of her hair caught in the stirrup as she swung the saddle up and over her horse.

"Ouch," she said in surprise. The ribbon tying her braid must have come unfastened during her ride. Irritably, she brushed her hair back murmuring, "I've got to cut this one of these days."

Finishing with the cinch, she ran her flashlight over him again. "Are you hurt?" she asked, concern in her voice. "Broken bones, bad lacerations?"

"No, no," he answered impatiently. "Just a few scrapes and bruises. Look, can we get out of here?"

"That's some gratitude," Sherri said lightly. "Now just relax, and everything will be all right. I'm trained to help out in these situations." She lapsed into the ranger speech that they all used to calm rescued people, then stopped. Barrett certainly didn't need her talk, and he would only think she was being sarcastic.

In silence she carefully moved her hands over his arms and legs, checking for broken bones. She noticed that he was ice-cold: the wet clothes were clinging to him and causing shivers up and down his body.

"I told you I was fine," he said with chattering teeth.

Sherri discovered a large bump on his forehead and nearly dropped the flashlight, remembering her fears about his possible drowning. "Were you unconscious?" she asked urgently.

"No, no concussion. I'm just freezing my rear end off. Please, Sherri, cut the ranger act and get us the hell out of here."

Sherri realized it was the first time he'd used her given name. But she couldn't think about that now. She still had to do her job. "Do you have any dry clothing at all?" she asked.

"Do you think I'd be wearing these wet things if I did?" Barrett asked incredulously. "I flipped the Land Rover, all right? Exactly the way you said I would. I soaked all my food, all my clothes, and every inch of my skin. The only thing I managed to keep dry was the walkie-talkie. So go ahead and say you told me so," he finished bitterly.

"You're in no state to listen to that right now," Sherri said in a brisk voice. She started to unbutton his shirt.

"What do you think you're doing?" he demanded, his teeth chattering as his icy hands grabbed at hers.

"I'm getting you undressed. Strip, and put these on." She untied the clothes from around her waist. "It's a sweat suit. I usually sleep in it, but it should be baggy enough to fit you."

"Oh, I get it. Well, I don't mind wearing your boyfriend's old clothes," Barrett said snidely, and Sherri gasped.

Suddenly all the joy she'd felt at seeing him alive had vanished. "After you change, leave your pack and all that wet gear. The horse can't carry our weight and that, too. We'll have to return for it tomorrow," she said in her most impersonal tone. Then she turned her back and mounted the saddled mare.

"Are you ready yet?" she asked into the dark.

"Yes."

"Then grab a change of clothes to dry out for tomorrow, give me your hand and mount up." For a moment, Sherri hated even the idea of touching him. But she reminded herself that she was a ranger and was not being paid to like the people she rescued. She was paid to take care of them as professionally as she knew how.

When Barrett had heaved himself onto the horse, Sherri told him, "Put your arms around me and move closer. I want as much of your weight forward on Bug as possible."

"Bug?" he repeated, obviously confused.

"Ladybug. The mare," she said in clipped tones. "Are you settled?"

"Yes, uh, thank you. Miss Landers—" he started to say, but Sherri cut him off.

"Look, right now you're just another job, so be quiet and let me do it in peace." She looked carefully around to fix the location of Barrett's pack in her memory, then she checked her watch. It was after nine-thirty. If they were lucky, and if the horse's energy didn't flag, they might make it back to the camp by one in the morning. The first hour didn't go badly; the terrain wasn't harsh, and there were now two flashlights to illuminate the way. By the second hour the mare, who had already put in a full day's work, was visibly beginning to tire.

Sherri quickly dismounted, and murmuring words of encouragement to the horse, continued on foot, the reins in her hand. Barrett started to dismount, too, but Sherri soon put a stop to that. He was not only cold and suffering from exposure, but worn out from his earlier hiking, weighed down with wet gear and a saddle. She also suspected blisters on his feet because of the wet socks and boots he'd been wearing. No, he would have to ride. She talked gently to the mare, promising her the next day off to rest. They would need that time to dry Barrett's clothes and sleeping bag, too. Sherri plodded forward, leading the horse. It was going to be a long night, and a very long walk.

Finally, much later, the mare nickered softly, and Sherri heard the answering whinny of Brownie, her gelding. Tomorrow, Brownie would have to backtrack for Barrett's gear. But now, it was past midnight, and she and Ladybug were exhausted. Barrett had to be in bad shape himself. If it wasn't such a cheap shot, Sherri would have taken great satisfaction in asking him if he still thought himself such an expert. People didn't realize how easy it was to die up here.

"Are we almost at the camp?" Barrett asked faintly. His voice was tinged with weariness, but Sherri had to give him credit; he hadn't complained the whole time. And he would have dismounted and walked beside her if she hadn't threatened to knock him out with her flashlight.

"Yes. How are you holding up? Is that head giving you any trouble?"

"Nothing a few aspirin won't cure. Don't worry, you won't have to evacuate me," he said, a trace of the old Barrett evident in his voice. Sherri felt relief at that. A good night's sleep and some warm clothing should fix his body up fine. Too bad it wouldn't improve his personality.

Sherri walked the horse right up to the tent. "Get off, and get into the sleeping bag," she commanded. "Toss me your boots. I'll see if I can dry them by the fire. And please don't argue with me."

Barrett did as he was told. "This is a double sleeping bag," he remarked.

"How very observant. Not only does it come in handy with all the men I entertain," she said sarcastically, "it even helps out on rescues when I have more than one person suffering from exposure. But don't worry, I won't be honoring you with any visits tonight. *Nothing* could induce me." With those stinging words, Sherri left the tent to see to the mare.

She watered the horse, then tied her near a bank of soft grass. Ladybug plopped happily to the ground and stretched out, enjoying a well-deserved rest.

"I'd take you over a Land Rover any day," Sherri complimented her fondly.

Next she relit the fire, then spread Barrett's wet clothing over the rocks nearby. She retrieved the boots she had left outside the tent and moved them close to the flames. Then she scraped the stew she'd cooked for dinner into a bowl and took it to Barrett.

"Here, eat this. I'll be back with your bread and some coffee as soon as the water boils."

Barrett sat up, and Sherri noted that a little healthy color had returned to his face. "Miss Landers, I . . ."

"I'll check your head after you eat, as long as you don't feel there's any urgency," Sherri cut in. "Now please excuse me."

Barrett might have been tired and bruised, but that didn't stop him from feeling annoyed at her refusal to speak to him. He unzipped the bag and threw back the covers to follow her, then stopped as he saw Sherri grab a roll of biodegradable camping toilet tissue. Muttering under his breath, he resigned himself to eating the stew alone.

Sherri had indeed grabbed the tissue, but not for the reason Barrett thought. She felt the onset of a crying jag, something that hadn't happened for a long time. The guilt she'd suffered over leaving Barrett and the subsequent anxious moments she'd endured while she searched for him had drawn her nerves to the breaking point. His comment about the oversize sweat suit had been the final straw. Better to get it out of her system in private than to risk the dam bursting in front of Barrett. How he would welcome the chance to humiliate her, especially as his own pride wasn't doing so well, thanks to her. And she had no intention of becoming another one of M. S. Barrett's female casualties.

Sherri dabbed her cheeks with the tissue. Two weeks alone with this man would surely drive her to drink, she thought ruefully. At least it was dark, and Barrett wouldn't be able to see the evidence of what he would probably call natural female weakness. He might have been able to bully all those other rangers, but he wasn't going to get the better of her. Sherri rose and strode purposefully toward the tent.

In spite of her tiredness, she was all business as she sat next to Barrett with the first-aid kit. The light of the lantern showed that it was almost one o'clock by Sherri's watch. She sighed and closed her eyes briefly, then continued cleaning the graze on Barrett's forehead.

"It's been an awful day, hasn't it?" Barrett echoed her unspoken thoughts, wincing as she scrubbed at a particularly ground-in piece of gravel.

Sherri said nothing; instead, she concentrated on placing a protective bandage over the graze.

"Aren't you going to say anything?" Barrett asked curiously. "Any other woman would be screaming 'I told you so' and rubbing it in deep."

Sherri gave him a look of scorn, unmistakable even in the dim light of the tent. "Your feet, please," was all she said.

"They're fine," Barrett replied.

"As fine as you said you were when you radioed in?" Sherri reminded him. "Or do you always misrepresent the facts?" She pulled down the zipper of the sleeping bag and yanked the closest leg onto her lap.

"Just as I thought," she said, ignoring the look of venom Barrett directed toward her. Sure enough, his foot was covered with ragged, broken blisters. Sherri clicked her tongue in dismay, and gently cleaned and dressed the raw areas, then reached for the other foot and did the same.

She carefully closed the first-aid kit and returned it to her pack. Overcome by a sudden fit of weariness, she rested her head on her knees. Her hair floated over her thighs, but Sherri was too exhausted to push it back. She was so tired, she thought to herself. So tired.

Barrett raised himself to a sitting position. "Did you have any dinner?" he asked.

"As if you care," Sherri mumbled.

Barrett frowned. "You gave me yours, didn't you?"

At that Sherri lifted her head and shrugged. "All in a day's work," she said lightly. Groaning aloud with weariness, she started pulling extra clothes out of her pack.

"What are you doing now?"

Sherri looked up at Barrett and noticed that his eyes were shadowed with tired smudges, as her own must have been. "I'm going to throw on some extra layers of clothes so I don't freeze tonight. I just put out the fire, and it won't be long before it gets really chilly in here."

"Oh, I get it," Barrett said with disdain. "You're going to prove what a good ranger you are and let me have the sleeping bag."

"I think you need it more than I do," Sherri said. "You can't sleep in yours, that much is certain. Besides, it appears I'm made of sterner stuff than you are. So in this case, I must bow to the weaker sex." Sherri couldn't resist the jab as she pulled on an extra sweat suit top. It fit easily over her other clothes, a fact that didn't go unnoted by Barrett.

"Then it's a good thing your boyfriend wears a big size," Barrett observed, "because you're going to need those clothes. If you think I'm going to do the gentlemanly thing and offer you this sleeping bag, you're sadly mistaken. You want to call the shots, lady; you'll have to live with the inconvenience."

Sherri paused a moment, then pulled on the sweatpants. In a small voice she said, "Those clothes are keeping you just as warm as they are me, so I'd appreciate it if you'd keep your rude comments to yourself. Not that it's any of your business . . . but they were my husband's. And as he can't use them anymore, I see no harm in my lending them out."

Barrett stared down at the gray material on his chest and fingered it. "He's dead?" he asked, his voice suddenly losing that arrogant quality.

"Good night, Barrett," Sherri said as she stretched out on the ground cloth, a flannel jacket tossed over her. "Turn off the lantern, would you?"

Sherri was so exhausted that even the hard ground felt good. She closed her eyes, waiting for the light to go off. Seconds passed, and she could still discern the white glow through her lids. Opening her eyes, she noticed that Barrett was still sitting.

"Are you in pain?" Sherri asked politely. "Your feet, maybe?"

Barrett shook his head.

"Then for heaven's sake turn off the light. I want to get some sleep." She closed her eyes again and relaxed.

"I'm sorry about your husband." Barrett's deep voice floated on the night air. "I didn't mean—" He stopped, then started again. "I shouldn't have made those nasty cracks."

Sherri refused to open her eyes. "Don't worry about it. The light, please." But it remained on, and wearily she rose on one elbow. "Now what?"

Barrett was getting out of the bag, maneuvering carefully to avoid injuring his feet any further. "I can't take your bed," he announced, his jaw resolutely set.

"Spare me your sacrifices," Sherri replied, sinking back on the ground. "If it makes you feel better, this whole mess is my fault. I broke the buddy-system rule because I agreed to our going separate ways. I didn't act like a professional, I acted like a headstrong child. I should have stuck with you no matter what. So now you can blame me for the whole thing and climb back into the sack. I'm too tired to argue anymore."

"You're taking the blame for this?" Barrett asked, his voice rising in astonishment.

"Someone has to. Go to sleep, Barrett," Sherri mumbled. "I'm not taking the sleeping bag."

Suddenly Sherri was jolted out of her drowsiness as her arm was grabbed and she was yanked into a sitting position. "Please, I want to go to sleep!" she cried piteously.

Barrett picked a leaf and some grass out of the tangled mass of cocoa hair. "The ground is too dirty to be sleeping on. Your hair is a mess."

Sherri jerked her arm away. "I usually braid it for the night, but I'm too tired! Just like I'm too tired for this nonsense. You're sleeping in that bed and that's final."

"There's an obvious solution," Barrett suggested.

Sherri laughed dryly. "No thanks," she said as she sank back onto the ground cloth, her hair spilling into the dirt. "I'd rather sleep with the horses."

Barrett reached over and gathered her up in his arms, then unceremoniously dumped her on the sleeping bag and knelt down beside her. For a man who had been through as much as he had, Barrett was surprisingly strong. Sherri whirled around to catch a strange, almost admiring glance on her captor's face.

"Anyone big enough to admit their errors deserves a reward," Barrett informed her. Bending low, he pressed his lips to hers.

Sherri's eyes were wide with astonishment as they fastened on Barrett's face. His kiss was sweet and gentle, she marveled, and her own lips softened involuntarily in response. In the dim light, Barrett's eyes glittered with some emotion Sherri couldn't identify, but that made no difference to the delicious feeling of contentment spreading through her body. She closed her eyes and eagerly reached up with her hands to feel those broad shoulders against her palms.

But to Barrett, her gesture seemed one of rejection, intended to rebuke him, to push him back, and he slowly leaned away from her. There was a long moment of uncomfortable silence.

Finally, Sherri gathered her wits about her. "What do you think you're doing?" she asked in a none-too-steady voice.

Barrett seemed just as shaken as she was, but a weak smile crossed his face as he said, "I must be concussed after all."

"You were born that way, mister," Sherri accused with tart conviction fueled by self-anger. How could she let him take her for granted so easily? "For the last time, good night." She turned off the lantern herself, and stretched comfortably in the downy softness of the sleeping bag.

Barrett carefully kept to his own side, and could soon hear Sherri's slow, even breathing. He thought she was asleep, and had almost drifted off himself when he felt her soft voice tickling his ear.

"What does the *M* stand for?" she suddenly asked.

"The what?" asked Barrett in confusion.

"The *M*, as in M. S. Barrett. What does it stand for?"

Barrett wasn't going to answer, but remembering all her concern for him and her attention to his injuries, he relented. "Miles. As in Miles Standish Barrett. And no, I don't want to hear any Pilgrim jokes."

"Miles..." Sherri rolled the name off her tongue and smiled in the darkness.

"Good night, Miles." Then she was asleep.

# CHAPTER THREE

THE SUN WAS STREAMING into the tent, its brightness and warmth causing Sherri to stir and waken. She groaned, then peeled off the outer layers of clothing, their removal a cooling relief. She noticed that the sleeping bag was open and the top half had been turned back. Barrett was gone. Her watch said it was almost eleven o'clock, and Sherri started guiltily. The horses had to be taken to the nearby stream and watered, then their pickets moved.

She rose and hurried out, her limbs stiff with sleep. Once outside the tent, she stopped in amazement. Coffee and bacon sat on the portable stove. The horses had been moved to a shady area, and judging by their playful behavior, they weren't suffering from thirst. The gear that had been left behind last night had been recovered. Barrett's clothes, along with his sleeping bag, were hung on a makeshift clothesline to dry.

Sherri sank weakly onto a large rock and pushed the tangled mass of hair away from her face. For a man who had so recently survived a near catastrophe, Barrett certainly bounced back quickly.

"About time you woke up," came a deep voice behind her.

With only the slightest of limps, Barrett strode past her and poured out a cup of coffee. "Here you are, Landers."

Sherri took it gratefully, grimacing as she tasted the unsugared brew. "Did you water the horses?" she asked, just to make sure.

"Of course," he said archly. "They couldn't wait for you to take care of them."

Sherri froze at the patronizing comment. Yes, she had slept uncharacteristically late, but he *could* have awakened her.

Abruptly she set down the coffee and turned to head back to the tent and a clean change of clothes. After all the trouble he had caused her yesterday, she fumed, Barrett now had the audacity to chastise her for not doing her share of the work.

She emerged from the tent with her toothbrush, soap and fresh clothes. Barrett still stood where she had left him, and she swept by, pointedly ignoring his presence.

"Landers?" he called out after her.

Sherri stopped and turned around, eyes narrowed. "What?"

"Here, you forgot this." He threw the roll of camping tissue at her with a mocking smile, and Sherri had to bite back an angry retort as she caught it.

Back rigid, she made her way to the stream for her morning's grooming. A quick wash did nothing to improve her temper, although the icy water, what there was of it, certainly refreshed her. But Sherri was worried about the low level of the stream and the dryness of the surrounding vegetation. She made a mental note to be extra careful with her fires, then toweled off and dressed. The clean clothing felt good against her skin, and as soon as she returned to camp, untangled her hair and had some breakfast, she'd be ready to tackle the day's problems. Or more accurately, tackle her problem partner.

Sherri had rinsed out yesterday's clothing in the stream, and now she hung it on the rope Barrett had strung between two trees. Although she knew he was watching her closely, she refused to acknowledge his presence. She pulled out her ranger's daily logbook, settling it on her lap to make yesterday's entry. But her pen froze above the page, and Barrett caught her hesitation.

"It's going to be a bit sticky for us, isn't it?" he asked her, his expression worried. "If we tell the truth, we might as well resign right now. You and I split up, against regulations. I lost the Land Rover, definitely a mark against me, and so far we've spent two days doing everything but our mapping assignment."

Sherri frowned, then flung the leather-bound tablet onto the ground with disgust. "Any suggestions?" she asked tartly.

"Yes. One, you settle down and have a cup of coffee and some breakfast. I promise to let you eat in peace," he cajoled at Sherri's scowl. "Maybe between the two of us we can cook up some story, though I see no way around reporting the damaged Land Rover." Barrett sighed, and despite herself, she felt almost sorry for him.

Barrett intercepted her soft look, and his lips turned down at the corners. "Just what I need, sympathy from the weaker sex," he said, rolling his eyes. "How about some eggs?" he asked lightly, but Sherri wasn't fooled.

Starting to work on her hair with a heavy brush, Sherri asked, "How hard would it be for you to get another job?"

Barrett snorted. "You've seen my personnel folder. I have a lousy track record. I was only hired with the state because I have veteran's preference, and even then they tried their best to pass me over. If I lose this job, I might as well go back to living off my relatives." He added water to the powdered egg mixture, then lit the stove.

"It's my own fault," he admitted reluctantly. "Oh, don't look so surprised. I know you didn't think I'd own up to my mistakes, but I can be just as righteous as you. This is the first time I've been proved wrong, though." He laughed bitterly. "Well, I promise to try and help you save your job, anyway. No sense in both of us going on welfare and adding to the taxpayer's burden." He beat the mixture savagely, but Sherri didn't miss the desolate expression in his eyes.

Sherri hated that bleak look, and something within her chest expanded. She didn't particularly like the man, but she could certainly identify with him. There must be a pool of bad luck somewhere that just waited to rain on people like her and Barrett.

"Look, things may not be so bad," she told him. Barrett looked up at her, his eyebrows raised in disbelief.

"No, I'm serious," she insisted. "First let me fix this mop of mine and have something to eat, and then we'll see what we can do about saving both our jobs. What time do we have to radio in?"

"Holden said sometime tomorrow morning," Barrett replied. He tried to damp down the rays of hope rising within him, but then something about this woman's assured, confident manner made him feel that perhaps his optimism wasn't misplaced. She'd been right once; maybe she'd be right again.

"Lady, if you can pull us out of this mess, you'll have my undying gratitude," he said frankly. "Let's hope you do better with our jobs than you're doing with that hair. Come on, give me the brush," he demanded, exasperated by her slow progress. "At this rate we'll be here all day."

Sherri hesitated, but he moved closer and firmly took the brush from her hand. Then his hands were on her head, gently making order of the snarled mass. At first Sherri tensed each time the brush caught in a tangle, but she soon realized that he wouldn't hurt her, and she began to relax with the soothing motions.

"There," he said. "Do you want your usual bun or one long braid?"

"That's all right," Sherri protested, uneasy at their sudden intimacy. "I can manage."

Barrett was annoyed at her refusal to decide, so he started to plait the long strands into one shiny braid. Sherri dug into her pocket and pulled out a leather strip with some brightly colored beads on it that she often used to fasten her hair when not on duty. Barrett silently finished his task, then stretched out a hand for the tie. He carefully placed it around the ends of her hair and knotted it securely.

Sherri reached back to check his work and noted that the braid was neither too tight nor too loose. "You've done this before," she said with conviction.

She couldn't see his face as he answered, "Yes, but it was a long time ago."

"I'm sorry," Sherri said softly. "Did she die, too?"

"No," Barrett answered bitterly. "No, she sent me a 'Dear John' letter while I was in the service and stationed overseas. She found someone else in my absence and married him. Better a sure thing than taking a chance on a military man, I guess." He shrugged. "The ironic thing is that my hitch was almost over and I had planned on coming home. Win some, lose some, I guess. But I don't intend to lose any more. I learned my lesson the hard way." He began to fry Sherri's eggs, and the expression on his face discouraged further comment.

Sherri watched him, wondering what kind of woman would abandon a man just because he was far from home. No wonder he avoided emotional entanglements—even friendship. Her reasons were as strong as his, though.

"I lost the love of my life to the military myself," Sherri said, not concealing her own regret.

Barrett looked up from his position in front of the frying pan. "You, too?"

Sherri nodded. "I met Thomas after I finished school. He was a career man with the Air Force."

Barrett waited as she paused, and after a second Sherri felt comfortable enough to go on. "He was a test pilot, a good one. But he was older than I was, and his reflexes were slowing down. Well, he had a chance at a good job teaching student pilots, but he refused it."

Barrett's face clouded with understanding. "He kept on flying against your wishes?"

"Don't you know it," Sherri spit out. "Sure enough, two weeks after he refused the teaching job, he was killed in a helicopter crash. The final verdict was pilot error." Sherri's voice dropped to a strangled whisper. "What a waste." Sherri gazed unseeing at the ground, the old sorrow mixing with surprise at her sudden outspokenness. She had never told anyone about Thomas's death before.

Barrett carefully scooped her eggs onto a plate, and added two pieces of bread. "I don't suppose you're in any mood to eat these," he said kindly, "but as you didn't have any dinner last night, you should make an effort. I'll go check on the horses," he finished, tactfully leaving her alone to regain control of herself.

Sherri wiped the tears from her eyes and stared at the plate of food Barrett had left on her lap. Taking several deep breaths, she tried to revive her lagging energy, concentrating on the task ahead. She was technically "on the clock," after all, and she wasn't being paid to mope around feeling sorry for herself. She forced herself to eat the eggs, then put away the plate and turned off the stove. Grabbing her canteen, some rope and her saddle, she set off in the direction of the horses.

"All through?" Barrett asked at her approach.

Sherri nodded. "Grab your rope and saddle the gelding. We have a Land Rover to attend to."

After one brief conversation with Barrett, during which he assured her that his head and feet weren't giving him any problems, the long ride back to the Land Rover was made in silence. Sherri didn't push the horses—their strength would be needed later—but she didn't dally on the journey, either. With only a few stops to rest the animals, and to allow her and Barrett to drink from their canteens, Sherri insisted on a steady pace.

When they finally arrived at the stream, the first thing Sherri noticed was the sun's reflection glinting off the side of the Land Rover. She sighed in despair; the situation was even more serious than she'd expected. Although the water was only ankle-deep the vehicle had mired down on its side, with every indication that it might fall further, overturning completely. At least Barrett had unhooked the horse trailer before he'd attempted to cross.

"Care to take back those brave words of earlier?" Barrett taunted, watching the expression on her face. At Sherri's silence, he added disgustedly, "I told you it was bad."

Sherri dismounted, took off her boots and waded out to the Land Rover. "With the horses, we should be able to get it back upright," she called out. "The biggest problem will be getting it out of the water." Sherri looked at the deep holes the tires had dug in the shale and mud, and sighed again, shaking her head.

"Would you stop with the sighs, already? Let's worry about one thing at a time." He started to dismount, but Sherri protested.

"Stay on the horse and save your feet. I can tie the ropes. Toss them over. Or are you going to start arguing again?"

Barrett frowned, but saw the wisdom of her words. He remained on the horse and threw her the ropes. It didn't take long for Sherri to fasten the ends, then she put on her boots and remounted.

"Do you have your end fastened securely to the saddle horn?" she asked.

"Of course I do. I'm not that stupid," Barrett answered indignantly.

"With your track record, forgive me for asking," was Sherri's dry response. "Ready? Steady pressure...now go!" She touched her heels to the mare's sides.

The Land Rover plopped onto all four wheels with a splash, and Sherri quickly released the tension on her rope, as did Barrett.

"You don't suppose it will start, do you?" she wondered aloud.

"Maybe later, after the engine dries out. There doesn't seem to be any major body damage except for those deep scratches from the shale and a few dents. But as for starting, I wouldn't even bother going to the trouble of turning the key. You might even short out the engine."

Sherri dismounted and retied the ropes to the back of the Rover. "Here's hoping," she muttered, crossing her fingers.

Both she and Barrett spurred the horses, but without success. The Rover would start to move, only to sink back into the mud. The horses were sweating now, and Sherri put a stop to their labors.

"We're so close," she said in frustration. "Just another few inches and we'd be on firmer ground. And just where do you think you're going?" she asked as Barrett suddenly dismounted and tossed her his reins.

"You look like a smart lady. I'll give you one guess."

Sherri flew out of the saddle to run in front of him and block his progress. "Oh, no, you don't, Barrett. You nearly killed yourself the last time you tried some fool stunt. I'm not going to watch you take a chance on falling under the truck. It would be so easy for the Rover to slide back and crush you, you...you idiot!'' Her voice rose to a crescendo. ''I'm senior ranger, and I forbid it!''

''Do you have any better suggestions?'' Barrett asked tersely.

''Yes. Why don't we just leave it here, for starters?'' Sherri proposed in a calm, sensible voice.

''I'll give you one good reason why not. U-N-E-M-P-L-O-Y-M...'' he started to spell until Sherri's restraining hand stopped him.

''Go ahead and push all you want, but these are my horses, and I'm not going to allow them to help you.''

Sherri turned to walk away, but Barrett grabbed her arm and jerked her around. His face was livid as he shook her. ''If I lose this job I'm as good as dead, partner, so you get your behind up on that horse, grab the gelding's reins and pull, you hear me?'' His broad hands shook her shoulders, emphasizing every word, and Sherri backed away from him in fear.

''You're crazy!'' Sherri accused him. ''Absolutely certifiable.''

''That may be,'' Barrett agreed, ''but you were the one who had me believing in your fairy tale of 'everything will be all right,' and you had better be prepared to deliver here and now!''

Sherri watched him wade into the water and position his hands on the far end of the Land Rover. ''I'm ready, now pull,'' he commanded in a whiplash of a voice, and Sherri trembled, but obeyed.

The Land Rover moved slightly, but as before, it started to slip back. Sherri saw Barrett push hard against the metal frame, his muscles bulging, his face tight. The Land Rover stayed put, and Sherri could tell that Barrett was losing the battle. Once more, she spurred the horses, but they were already at the limit of their strength. Suddenly the Land Rover started to slide back again.

''Barrett!'' Sherri screamed. She gave the mare a stinging slap with her reins and screamed ''Yaah, Brownie,'' at the top of her lungs. The vehicle lurched, the horses stumbled forward, and five seconds later the Land Rover sat on dry land.

Barrett stumbled to the shore and sank to the ground to steady his trembling knees. Sherri would have joined him, but she was shaking so badly, she was afraid she'd fall if she tried to get down. Instead she turned halfway around and guiltily rubbed at the welt on Ladybug's flank.

"Are you okay?" she was finally able to ask.

Barrett looked up and nodded. "I'm in better shape than the mare," he said, and Sherri thought she heard condemnation in his voice.

"I never hit a horse in my life until today! You almost got yourself killed, and if it wasn't for these horses and my abusing them, you would have been! I should have let you fall under the Rover! Ladybug is worth twenty of you," she said, her voice trembling.

Barrett rose and yanked her off the horse. He crushed her against him and bending his head, covered her lips with his, silencing her outburst. Mindful of his blistered feet, he sank to his knees, and then to the ground, all the while bringing Sherri with him. His kiss seared and burned, taking her breath away. She opened her mouth to protest, and Barrett took the opportunity to deepen the kiss.

Sherri knew she should fight back harder, but the suddenness of his onslaught, coupled with shock, immobilized her at first. Then something else prevented her from resisting more forcefully. Feelings she hadn't experienced in a long, long time started to awaken. Awareness of herself as a woman, instead of just a hard-working ranger, began to surface. Sherri groaned that the igniting of her dormant passions should be accomplished by a man she didn't even like, but Barrett took her groan for consent, and his actions became even bolder.

One hand slipped inside her shirt to travel over the smooth curve of a breast, while the other untied the leather of her braid and unbound her hair. He brought the silky strands to his lips and murmured, "You should never cut it, never..."

It wasn't until he started to unbuckle her belt that Sherri came to her senses and fought against the treacherous tide her body was drifting on. A strong woman, she struggled out from beneath him and quickly backed away.

"Just what do you think you're doing?" she gasped as she pushed back the cloud of hair floating around her face.

Barrett didn't look disturbed at all. "Why, calming a hysterical woman," he answered offhandedly. "Of course, I could have slapped you, but this was much more fun." He rose to his feet and brushed at the debris sticking to his muddy jeans.

"If that's the way you act with your partners, it's no wonder all the women were begging to be reassigned," Sherri sputtered as she moved even farther away from him to rebuckle her belt. Then she picked up the leather tie from the ground and used it to pull her hair into a ponytail.

"For a man who nearly got himself killed twice in two days, you don't seem too concerned about it." Her voice was scornful. "I know your type."

"And just what type is that?" Barrett asked casually, but his eyes were wary and waiting.

"You're the type who can't enjoy the simple life," Sherri accused. "I know; I was married to a man like you. He thrived on danger. You don't look on it as a necessary job risk, like I do. My husband is dead because he couldn't enjoy the everyday pleasures. A calm, peaceful life with me just wasn't enough. The two of you were cut from the same cloth!"

"How dare you," Barrett hissed.

"I dare, because I know. Thomas lived his life as one great adventure. Better to die gloriously than live a dull life, that was his motto. Just like you, Barrett. So you keep your kisses to yourself, because I've buried one man like you already. I have no intention of doing it again." Sherri was shaking as she mounted Ladybug. What had triggered the release of that dam of bitterness?

Barrett was silent as he caught the gelding's reins and swung himself into the saddle, but he managed to have one last say. Eyes deadly, he looked at her hard. "If you ever dare to psychoanalyze me again and spout such insulting rubbish to my face, partner or no partner, job or no job, I'll break your lovely neck." He spurred his horse and took the lead back to the camp this time, leaving Sherri to follow or not, as she pleased.

It was close to evening when they reached the camp. Barrett busied himself repacking all his dried gear, while Sherri tended to the horses. She apologized profusely to the mare for the injury, and felt better after she shrank the size of the welt with cold compresses.

Sundown soon arrived, and Barrett turned on the radio to call the base. Sherri had to marvel at the coolness of his tone as he requested that the Land Rover be picked up. "Yes, I'm afraid I damaged the paint somewhat. Those horses of Sherri's starting acting up and swinging the trailer around. I'm afraid I sideswiped a few trees, but other than that the Rover is fine. I left the keys in the glove compartment. We won't be needing it anymore—or the horse trailer either."

Sherri wondered how he could keep a straight face at the lies, but at least he'd blamed the damage on the horses, and he and Sherri were in the clear. She fervently hoped the vehicle's ignition would dry off enough to start.

Sherri listened to Holden's voice crackling on the other end. "And what do you have to report for mapping coordinates?" Holden asked.

Barrett was momentarily at a loss, and Sherri took the opportunity to pluck the microphone from his hand. "We've made quite a bit of progress these past two days," she began. Barrett stared at her, then leaned closer, curious to hear how she was going to handle this one.

"We've scouted out two, possibly three future trails for the parks. Do you have a pen and paper handy? Good, I can transmit them right now." From memory, she reeled off coordinates and land descriptions faster than Holden could jot them down. Barrett was plainly astonished, Holden himself pleased.

"Well, Landers, I have to admit that I thought you and Barrett would have been at each other's throats by now. It's refreshing to see you two can work together." Holden's deep baritone chuckle rumbled over the line. "Although I imagine it hasn't been easy. Any problems?" he inquired.

Sherri handed the microphone to Barrett. She had done her part, and he was certainly a better liar than she was. Let him sweat it out, she thought.

"Nothing we can't handle," Barrett said smoothly.

Holden sounded instantly suspicious. "Come, come, surely you don't expect me to believe that?"

"Well, I do object to my partner's sleeping in all the time. And I had to reprimand Landers for the way she treated one of the horses. But she seemed to take my criticism fairly well." Barrett's eyes twinkled wickedly as Sherri drew an indignant breath.

Grabbing the microphone from him, she added "What can I say, boss? My boy scout of a partner here blistered his feet hiking in wet boots, and I had to overwork my horse because the fool couldn't walk. As for sleeping late, well, what can you expect? The man practically sobbed on my shoulder all night over a few blisters. It's no wonder I had to catch up on my sleep in the morning. Still, I suppose I have no choice but to manage," Sherri concluded, not daring to look at Barrett's face.

"Hmm," was all Holden would say. "However, I'm extremely pleased with your surveying work so far. In fact, I'm so pleased that I'm willing to overlook the minor damage to the Land Rover. Keep up the good work, and you might—just might—be able to bank on your next pay check. Over and out."

Barrett shut off the radio, then stood gazing at Sherri in disbelief, while she slowly expelled the breath she didn't know she'd been holding. They had done it!

Barrett let out a slow whistle. "Lady, I don't know how you pulled that off. If those coordinates are correct—" Sherri nodded enthusiastically "—then we're off the hook!" Their eyes met in a quick smile of satisfaction—and relief.

Suddenly, he raised one eyebrow. "I sobbed on your shoulder?" he quoted.

"I can't make it out of bed in the morning?" Sherri threw back at him, her arms crossed over her chest.

There was another moment of silence. Barrett shook his head, then impulsively let out a cheerful whoop. "We're still on the payroll!"

Sherri was taken aback by how much younger and more attractive his face appeared when he was laughing.

"You'd better show me where the rest of those trails are," Barrett said, still smiling, "or I'm going to seem pretty ignorant. We *are* going to do some actual surveying, aren't we?"

"Oh, yes. I have a pretty fair idea of our plans for the next few days, but we won't need to do any blind exploring. I know my way around. It's simply a matter of checking out new rockslide areas, washouts, you know, your average topographical changes." Sherri laced her hands behind her head and sighed contentedly. "In fact, if it weren't for you, these two weeks would be a restful vacation."

Barrett appraised her thoughtfully. "You knew those coordinates all along," he accused. "You let me worry my head off about losing my job, and you had the information down pat all the time!"

Sherri smiled. "I told you to trust me," she said smugly. "Is it my fault you erred by relying only on yourself?" She savored her triumph. For a moment she wondered if Barrett was going to show her his temper again. But he merely glared at her, hands shoved into his pockets.

"Landers," he warned.

"Barrett," she answered with a grin.

"Well, you did save my job," he admitted ruefully, "so I won't quibble about your typical female secretiveness. I will, however, cook your dinner. That's the least I can do."

"No more powdered eggs," she shouted after him, then laughed at the insulted look he gave her. She felt so much better now that the first radio call to Holden was over. That queasy feeling in the middle of her stomach was gone, and she realized just how much she had feared losing her job.

Barrett was true to his word. Not only did he cook their dinner on the portable stove, but he lit a cozy fire to keep them company.

"Hey, this is really great!" Sherri marveled. "How did you make canned food taste so good?"

Barrett shrugged. "I always had a flair for cooking, and I enjoy good food. Canned stuff certainly doesn't fall into that category, so I started experimenting with spices and herbs to try and pep it up. You are eating the results of hundreds of cans of experience," he announced with a touch of pride.

"You'll have to give me the recipes," Sherri insisted after swallowing another tasty bite. "The only thing I don't enjoy about camping is the canned and dried food. It's awful. I'm glad to learn it doesn't have to be that way," she said with grudging admiration. Her own meals never tasted this appetizing.

They continued eating in companionable silence.

"How did you come to know these mountains so well, Sherri?" Barrett asked, using her first name as naturally as if they'd always been friends.

"I grew up here," Sherri answered, wondering if she dared call him Miles.

"But how? There aren't any towns around. Even the ranger station is fairly recent." She didn't reply, and Barrett pressed her for an answer. "Please, Sherri, I'd really like to know."

She hesitated, not certain if he was interested or only making polite conversation. Still, she was willing to talk. So Sherri told him about her prospecting father, her early years with her mother, and how she came to consider the mountains her home. "I ended up with the rangers, and here I am, back in the same place I started," Sherri concluded. "Sometimes it seems as if I've never left, and my time with Thomas was just a dream."

Barrett pondered the strange story. "And you never heard from your father again?" he asked.

"No, I'm afraid not. We had . . . still have a cabin way up in the high country. My father filed a claim on the land when I was just a baby. On my vacations I ride up to see if he's stopped in and maybe left me a note, but he hasn't. All the notes I've left him are still there. He's probably been dead for years. I wish I knew for sure. He's the only family I have." Sherri's eyes grew wistful at her memories of the man who had been such a harsh taskmaster, yet had loved her and taken care of her in his own way.

Barrett started to say something about how lonely she must have been, but stopped himself. She wouldn't welcome his pity any more than he would welcome hers. He noticed that her voice had gone a little husky when she spoke again, interrupting his thoughts.

"Now it's your turn. You tell me something about yourself."

Barrett added more wood to the fire before he settled down to answer. "I'm from a larger family than yours. I have a married brother, and a younger sister. My parents are still happily married, and everyone seems to be doing well. I have two nephews but don't get home to see them often enough, I suppose," he said sadly.

"Where are you from?"

"Portland. My father's in the fishing industry. I hate the smell of raw fish—" he grimaced "—almost as much as I hate being seasick." He admitted his weakness reluctantly. "I had planned to go to college, but I decided to join the military instead and see something of the world first. When I came back, my girlfriend Karen was married and pregnant, so I went to an out-of-state college to get away from home and from her. I never went back, and I suppose I've drifted about ever since."

Barrett tossed more sticks into the flames and then continued. "This job was a godsend. There was enough action in it to keep me occupied, and enough remoteness to satisfy my desire to be left alone."

"Except for your partners," Sherri tacked on.

"They wouldn't leave me alone," Barrett said, sounding almost embarrassed. "They reminded me of my sister, always trying to mother me and make me feel better. What with losing the woman I'd planned to marry, I wasn't in the mood for all those soft shoulders to cry on."

"Was that any reason to take your frustrations out on them? That's what you were doing, wasn't it?" Sherri's voice came softly out of the fading light.

Barrett shrugged. "Didn't you do the same thing to your partners?" he countered.

Sherri refused to answer that, but her silence was a tacit admission. For a while there was no sound but the crackle of the flames and the popping of wood.

"I suppose I should go check on the horses," Sherri said at last.

"I'll go," Barrett offered. "I owe you one. No, even more than that," he said. He made no move to get up, though, and the two of them watched the night darkness roll in.

"I think I'll get to sleep early," Sherri told him. "It's been a long day, and I'd like us to get an early start tomorrow. Are you coming to bed soon?" she asked, wondering if she should keep the lantern burning. They would have to share her tent again, since his had been lost when the vehicle overturned.

"No, I think I'll stay up for a while after I check the animals."

"Well, good night, then."

"Good night. And Sherri, I'm sorry about earlier today. My behavior was inexcusable. I do know how to act like a civilized human being, or at least I did once, a long time ago. I just need a little practice." Barrett didn't turn her way, and Sherri was at a loss for words.

Finally for lack of anything else to say, she brought up something that had been puzzling her. "How did you ever end up with a name like Miles Standish?"

Sherri heard his dry chuckle in the darkness. "I was wondering when you'd get around to that. Would you believe my sister's name is Felicity Prudence? Let's just say my father is a bit of a snob about our being descended from the Mayflower."

"Oh. Well, good night, Miles." She grinned a little at using his name, and felt rather than saw his answering grin in the darkness.

"Good night, Landers."

# CHAPTER FOUR

FOR THE SECOND TIME, Sherri woke up to an empty tent. She remembered seeing Barrett's outline through the nylon walls of her tent before drifting off to sleep. Not only hadn't she heard him finally come to bed, but she hadn't heard him rise, either. Barrett was obviously a man who didn't need much sleep; he was certainly an earlier riser than Sherri.

Sherri knew she wasn't at her best in the mornings, and she also suspected Barrett of enjoying that fact. Sure enough, as soon as she emerged from the tent, his first words were, "It's about time."

Sherri squinted at her watch, trying to focus the fuzzy hands into revealing the time. It was after seven, not that late, but still later than her usual waking time. Barrett was already dressed and cleanly shaved.

He held the camp tissue in one hand and a cup of coffee in the other. "Which will it be, sleeping beauty?" he inquired.

Sherri threw him a venomous look. "I don't find your vulgarity any more welcome than I do the taste of your horrendous coffee," she told him flatly.

Barrett shrugged, not offended. "I'd hardly classify normal bodily functions as vulgar. And there's nothing wrong with my coffee."

Sherri peered into the blackness of her cup and shuddered. "In this case, it's an easy choice," she murmured as she reached for the tissue.

"My feelings are crushed," Barrett sang out after her, and Sherri had the sneaking suspicion he was laughing at her. How she hated people who woke up bright and chipper! It was positively indecent.

She checked on the horses as she hurried to the stream and was piqued to see that they were happily munching away, having been recently moved. Unquestionably, Barrett was showing her up when it came to doing his share of work in the camp. Except for that first night, he had cooked all the meals, then taken care of the livestock and even made all the coffee. Well, Sherri thought with some satisfaction, after his poor performance at the beginning of their trip, he had a long way to go toward redeeming himself, in her eyes, anyway. If doing simple camp chores made him feel better, so be it. She didn't mind being the recipient of his bounty. That thought did much to brighten her morning, and Sherri strolled back to the camp with color in her cheeks and a smile in her eyes.

"Ready for breakfast?" asked Barrett as she returned, presenting her with a plate of steaming pancakes.

Sherri looked at them suspiciously. They certainly smelled good, but how could anything concocted with powdered milk, flour and powdered eggs taste credible?

"Come on, be adventurous," Barrett urged, understanding her hesitation. "Or would you rather have powdered scrambled eggs?"

Sherri shuddered with distaste, and quickly reached for the plate. Barrett poured on some syrup from little foil packets, and watched with amusement as she took her first bite.

"You remind me of a child trying her first piece of broccoli. It won't bite, little girl, so eat up."

Sherri glanced at him out of the corner of her eyes. Then, amazed to discover how delicious the pancakes actually were, she dug in greedily. When she finally came up for air, she asked, "How in the world do you manage these?"

Barrett lifted up his own plate for another serving. "Oh, no, you don't. A good chef never reveals his recipes. I just have the knack, I guess." He smiled, a maddeningly superior smile that Sherri couldn't quite bring herself to take offense at.

She started to ask another question, but suddenly closed her mouth.

"Well, what is it?" Barrett had noticed her expression, his sharp eyes missing very little.

"Nothing. I was going to ask you if Karen taught you to cook, but thought better of it." Sherri rinsed her plate and packed it away. "Thanks for breakfast."

"Why not ask? Most women would be curious to hear all the sordid details of a broken romance," Barrett observed. There was a sarcastic edge to his voice.

"Not me," Sherri denied uneasily.

"Come on, admit it, you're curious," he insisted with infuriating certainty.

"I'm not, truly," Sherri protested, but in spite of her words she had to confess that she *was* curious. What kind of woman would a man like Miles Barrett desire? With a start she realized that the subject had become unexpectedly intriguing.

Barrett saw her guilty look and pounced on her like a cat. "What a little liar you are."

"Why don't you just leave me alone?" Sherri snapped. "There's no being polite to you, is there?"

Suddenly upset, Sherri headed for the tent to repack the toilet articles and soiled clothing that she'd brought back from the stream. She always managed to say the wrong thing around Barrett, and already the day was off to a bad start. Sherri rubbed her forehead in frustration; she dreaded having to face him again but knew she couldn't hide in the tent forever. She sat cross-legged on the dirt, noticing that Barrett had even rolled up her sleeping bag.

She squinted at the bright glare of sunlight as Barrett parted the side of the tent and peered in. "Are you going to stay in here all day?" His words were brisk, bearing no resentment that Sherri could detect. "Come on, let's break camp, pack up and get moving. You can fill me in on our new coordinates as we work," he said in an all-business tone.

Sherri breathed a sigh of relief. After a few minutes she found the courage to join in the work, thankful that he wasn't going to hold her lapse in civility against her. Sooner than she thought possible, they were packed and the horses saddled. Then they set off.

It promised to be yet another clear, dry day. The weather all summer had been dry, and the woods and higher timberline looked rather wilted and faded, but beautiful just the same. With careful politeness, Sherri had outlined their day's proposed progress on the map before they left, and Barrett, equally polite, had agreed to her suggestions.

They rode in single file, Sherri leading on the mare. The quiet of the high mountain air would have made conversation quite easy in spite of the distance between their horses, but neither one of them seemed in the mood for conversation. Sherri contented herself with talking to her horse occasionally, and with glancing behind her from time to time to check on Barrett's progress. He seemed an experienced enough rider, and as Brownie had been over the landscape before, Sherri saw no need to interfere.

The sun started to get hot, and as she pulled her hat even further down on her face, she heard Barrett ask. "Do you want to take a breather?"

She merely nodded her response and headed over to a shady grove of aspens, their white-barked limbs promising a cool haven. Moments later, they were both swallowing water from their canteens as the horses nibbled at the ground.

"What I wouldn't give for a huge glass of soda on ice." Sherri sighed as she capped the canteen. The boiled stream water with its metallic taste from the canteen was, at best, a dubious pleasure.

"Do you realize those are the first words you've spoken to me all morning?" Barrett asked, taking another drink from his own container.

Sherri stood up and hung her canteen back on Ladybug's saddle. "I wasn't aware you were all that fond of my conversation," she said frankly. "Besides, I'm used to people not wanting my company." She stated the fact bluntly, without self-pity. "Why should you be any different?"

Sherri didn't see Barrett frown as she moved away from him and past the horses. His eyes were thoughtful as he watched her climb to a high point to survey the area. The wind loosened strands of hair and blew them about her face, and one delicate hand shielded her eyes from the sun. Cursing, Barrett rose to his feet. Of all the women he had been partnered with, she was proving the hardest for him to dislike. Being the prettiest of the batch, and the most capable in the wilderness, didn't help either.

They continued their work until noon. Sherri led the way, while Barrett carefully made notations on the map. The sun was directly overhead as Sherri guided them to water, then unsaddled the mare.

"I take it we're stopping here," Barrett remarked.

"The horses and I are," Sherri answered tartly. "You can do what you please." She noticed Barrett's flash of anger at her flippancy and felt strangely guilty. On the long ride up, she had decided that the only way for the two of them to get along was to avoid any intimacy, yet antagonizing Barrett didn't seem to make her feel better at all.

"I'm sorry," she said tentatively.

"Don't bother." Barrett uncinched the gelding, then tossed the saddle on the ground with little regard for the leather. "Why say it if you don't mean it?"

Sherri unsaddled Ladybug and placed her saddle on the ground with more care. Her face was turned away from him as she said, "You stopped those two rangers from making fun of me at the camp when we were leaving," she said slowly. "I know their taunts didn't bother you, but you got rid of them anyway. I really was grateful. I should be polite to you for that reason alone." Her voice was odd and stiff, but she held herself proudly as she apologized to him again. "Please forgive my rudeness."

Barrett paused at her words. "Don't worry about it," he said gruffly. "My manners aren't the greatest either," he admitted, strangely affected by the aura of vulnerability surrounding his partner. She had loved too deeply, he thought with a sudden flash of insight, wondering just how much of that love had been taken for granted by her husband. People as giving as Sherri, as honest, always seemed to get hurt. It was no wonder she had retreated into a shell.

"Let's call a truce," he offered. "No one at the camp has to know." He winked in an exaggerated gesture, and despite herself, Sherri smiled.

"Truce," she agreed, momentarily clasping his large hand with her own. "If only Holden could see us now," she added.

"I wouldn't give that so-and-so the satisfaction," Barrett growled, wishing he could say aloud the profanity he had disguised for Sherri's sake. "So, are you hungry?" he asked. "I can whip you up a gourmet special in a hurry."

"Not really. Those pancakes of yours are lying in my stomach like lead," she complained.

"I can only take credit for the taste, not for their effects on the digestion. Even I can't alter the fact that they're plain old C-rations, after all. What do you have in mind for this after noon?"

Sherri's face grew serious. "I don't like the smell or feel of that wind shift. We may be in for a rip-roaring storm."

Barrett scoffed at her fears. "We haven't had any good rainstorms all summer. In fact, the fire hazard is climbing."

Sherri shook her head in disagreement. "We may not get any precipitation, but I tell you we're in for a good storm, just the same."

Barrett sniffed the air again and watched the horses do the same. "With the dryness of the vegetation, an electrical storm is the last thing we need. One good stroke of lightning and we'd all be in for a merry time," he muttered, his eyebrows drawn with concern.

"Right now, I'm more worried about what the wind coming off the mountains during a storm will do to our nylon tent," Sherri said, picturing a cold, unsheltered night for the two of them. "I think we should skip lunch, saddle up again and ride due north."

Barrett stopped in the action of picking up his saddle. "Due north? Sherri, there's nothing up there but a few pine trees and rocks! Not to mention the sheer cliffs and drop-offs."

Sherri pulled on the mare's reins and urged her closer. "My cabin is up there. I hope I'm wrong, but I have a strong feeling we're going to need it."

The next few hours proved Sherri correct. Black clouds started rolling in, and the wind rose significantly. As the horses ascended the steep climb toward the north, Barrett became more and more anxious. He had always been a leader, not a follower, and to find himself behind a woman navigating seemingly sheer rock faces did nothing to soothe his nerves. If it weren't for Sherri's confident manner, and the gelding's obvious familiarity with the faint trail, he would have turned back more than once.

There was no sunset that evening; the blackness of the clouds soon obliterated first the sun, then the tops of the peaks. Sherri hated the exposed feeling of being on the bleak, rocky slopes. She knew they were almost at their destination, but still, she was nervous, and wondered at the steadiness of Barrett's nerves. Not only had he followed her without question, but he had trusted the judgment of a woman he barely knew. Sherri couldn't think of any other ranger she'd been partnered with who wouldn't have demanded detailed explanations from her.

Lightning danced across the sky, and both horses recoiled at the bright flashes. Sherri turned around and had to yell above the roar of the wind to make herself heard. "Just fifteen more minutes and we should be there," she screamed, brushing away the swirl of hair that veiled her face.

Barrett waved to show he'd heard her. Although his face remained impassive, he was grateful for her information. He didn't like the looks of those thunderclouds any more than Sherri did, and the ferocity of the wind indicated a quickly moving storm front.

The horses knew they were close to home now and eagerly pulled themselves and their riders up the steep incline. Sherri bent over in the saddle and hugged the mare's neck, offering reduced resistance to the wind. She hoped Barrett would follow her example, for the horses didn't need to be guided. Another streak of lightning eerily lit up the clouds before them, and Sherri trembled. She was getting more frightened by the minute.

The ground suddenly leveled, signaling the boundary of the cabin compound. Sherri rode to the corral and dismounted. She opened the gate for Barrett and the gelding, who were close behind her, then quickly led the horses into the makeshift stable. Barrett grabbed both packs and headed for the house while she unsaddled the horses. The animals were jittery, and Sherri decided to water them later. She had no intention of going anywhere in this storm except straight to the cabin.

Flashes of lightning illuminated her way as she ran into the cabin. Barrett slammed the door behind her, but they could still hear the thunder and the rushing of the wind.

"Did you take care of the horses?" Barrett asked in a loud voice.

"No," Sherri yelled. "There's no hay in the barn. They'll have to graze tomorrow."

He held cupped hands to his mouth and shouted, "What about water?"

"There's a pump behind the house, but I'm not going out again," she yelled back above the shrieking of the wind. "They'll just have to wait until the storm is over."

"They must be thirsty!" Barrett darted his flashlight around the room, then reached for a dusty bucket. "They got me up here in one piece, the least I can do is water them. You start a fire," he called out. "I'll be right back."

He walked out the door as though he were going for a Sunday stroll. *You're a better man than I am, Gunga Din,* Sherri thought with admiration. Or a crazier one. She shivered as another flash of lightning, so close at this altitude, heralded a booming clap of thunder.

A pile of firewood was faintly visible in the corner, but Sherri knew her way around the cabin by heart. The room was snug, the wood was dry, and before long a steadily blazing fire flooded the walls with soft light. Sherri added a last log for good measure and stood up, then suddenly froze. Every Christmas she had placed a card and letter for her father on the cabin's mantelpiece. The envelopes had piled up with the years, but Sherri had left them there, hoping that someday her father would return and know that she was thinking of him. But now, the mantelpiece was covered with nothing but dust.

Sherri searched frantically for an answering message. In the hazy light, she couldn't see anything remotely resembling a letter, and her search grew more frenzied.

"What's going on?" Barrett asked as he entered the room. "You're more skittish than the animals!"

Sherri whirled around. "The letters are gone! All of them!"

Barrett put his hands on her shoulders and halted her erratic movement. "Wait a minute, calm down!" he said, as if gentling the horses. "What letters?"

Sherri explained as coherently as she could. "I told you how I wrote him letters and brought them here, remember?" When Barrett nodded, she said again, "They're gone! That means he must have left me a note somewhere—but I can't find it! And it's so dark!" she wailed.

Barrett dug out a second flashlight from the pack and slapped it into her hand. "You start on the left half of the cabin, I'll start on the right. If we do this systematically, we'll have better results. Okay?"

Sherri nodded her agreement.

"Let's get started, then," Barrett said calmly, as if there weren't a storm waging outside, as if they weren't tired and hungry, as if looking for messages in the dark were a common occurrence.

Following his lead, Sherri drew a deep calming breath and began to look in a more orderly fashion. In spite of his abrasive personality, Barrett was a reassuring man to have around.

Barrett was the one to find the faded envelope marked "Sherri." He silently handed it to her and Sherri clasped the letter to her chest, then carefully stuffed it in her pocket.

"I suppose we'd better start fixing dinner," Sherri ventured in a shaky voice.

"I can wait, if you want to read that," Barrett responded.

"No. No, I was just worried that he might not have left a note. I'll dust and make this place presentable if you want to do your magic with the C-rations." Sherri did not add that she wanted to be alone when she read the letter, but he immediately seemed to grasp her meaning.

"If you wish," he said evenly, and Sherri was thankful that he asked no questions and made no comment.

Sherri was barely aware of what she ate. The letter burned like a flame in her pocket, and the ferocity of the storm created a strange, surrealistic atmosphere. From time to time Barrett would glance her way, as if checking on her, but Sherri didn't notice. After dinner, she busied herself with straightening up and unpacking the clothes she would need for the night, laying them on the little bed that had been hers from childhood.

Barrett unpacked his own things and sat down on her father's bed to update the log they were required to keep. Sherri watched him in silence for a while, then went about refastening the faded curtain that her father had hung so long ago to give her privacy. She sat dreamily on her bed, waiting for the storm to end. Gradually the thunder abated, and the clouds started to thin, so that some of the stars became visible. Sherri uncrossed her legs and got up to retrieve one of the flashlights.

"I'm going to let the horses graze now," she informed Barrett. "I'll be back in a bit."

Barrett nodded and resumed his work on the day's journal. Both of them knew why Sherri wanted to be alone.

The horses' shapes made dark silhouettes in the night as Sherri perched on a tree stump next to the corral. She hung the lantern on a fence post, and carefully opened the letter. It had been written last February, almost six months ago. For a minute her eyes blurred with happiness at the familiarity of her father's handwriting, then she was able to focus again and read.

My dearest daughter, I must thank you for all those kind letters and cards. I know you thought I never saw them, but, in fact, I read them soon after you left them for me.

Sherri lowered the paper for a moment. Whatever could he mean by that?

Of all the regrets in my life, the greatest has been the unorthodox childhood I forced on you after your mother's death. When she died, something in me died, too. I felt at peace up here in the mountains, and if I never found much gold, at least I enjoyed the hunt.

Sherri smiled at her father's rolling prose. He had been a well-educated man, something you wouldn't have guessed from his scruffy appearance.

To my profound unhappiness, I noticed that you were becoming too much like me. Solitary, alone… I was so happy when you got married. I wish I could have been there, but thought it best to absent myself from your life. And that year your husband died, and you returned to the cabin for a time, I was so deeply sorry for you. I know I wasn't around much, wasn't much help, but your grief reminded me too painfully of what I felt after your mother's death. I couldn't face it again. That seems selfish, but I also knew that I should leave you to get on with your mourning and give you a chance to resume your life. You were young enough to start over. Not like me.

When you left to join the rangers, I felt a great sense of happiness and relief. I didn't want to interfere with your new life and I didn't want you to feel any obligation toward me, so I kept away whenever you rode up here. But I read all your letters and resealed them to deceive you. I used to watch you and long to put my arms around you, but I feared that you would want to stay with me. And that just wouldn't have been right. It wouldn't have been fair to let a young woman, in the prime of her life, while away her days in this kind of isolation.

Sherri cursed her father's devotion to her, yet understood it all the same.

I saw you in your ranger's uniform a few times. My, was I proud of my little girl. You're very lucky to have the best of both worlds, Sherri. The company of others and the great outdoors, too.

Sherri blinked away a tear, glad her father had never known just how little of the company of others she had enjoyed. She read on.

I suppose you're wondering why I'm writing now, after all these years. I'm sorry to have to tell you that I'm not well. Guess I'm just getting old, baby. It's been a hard life up here, but for me, it's been a good one, too. I probably won't live through the winter, but I do have enough consideration for my dear girl not to have her walk in and find the body of her old man mouldering on the floor.

Sherri gave an anguished cry that carried up to the cabin. With shaking hands she tried to steady the paper so she could finish reading it.

When the end gets near, I'll stroll to our favorite spot. You know, the one your mother liked so well. I wish I could be buried next to her, but Sherri, if you can't handle it, that's okay. Just leave me where I am, to help the trees grow strong, and remember that I always loved you.

Tears were streaming down Sherri's face as she stumbled over the last page. It was her father's last will and testament, leaving to her the cabin and the land, which were all that he owned. He'd also left her some gold and silver.

I know it isn't much to show for thirty years of prospecting but it's all I have to leave you. You'll know where to look for it. Maybe you can go back to school or buy some pretty things for my grandchildren, if I ever have any. Remember that I always loved you, as did your dear mother, and remember that love is the only thing worth looking for, and living for. The rest is just so many dead leaves in autumn. I love you, Sherri.

The letter was signed, "Your father."

Sherri bowed her head, motionless save for the tears running slowly down her cheeks. That was how Barrett found her.

"Sherri?" He laid a gentle hand on her shoulder, but Sherri didn't move. Silently he tugged the papers out of her hand, then glanced quickly through the letter.

"Oh, Sherri." His breath came on a sigh, like a soft breeze. He slid the pages back into the envelope and carefully returned it to Sherri's hands.

"I'm so sorry." He placed one arm around her shoulders and drew her to her feet. "Let's go inside," he suggested.

"No!" Sherri froze, her face urgent. "I can't leave him outside all night! He'll be cold!"

Barrett gently swung her around to face him. "Sweetheart, it's late. We can't do anything tonight. Let's go in," he repeated.

Sherri looked up at him, her eyes dulled with anguish. "What if it rains? He'll get wet. He catches cold so easily..." Her voice broke as she tried to pull away from him.

Barrett's lips pressed together in a thin line. "Sherri," he tried again, "I know it hurts, but another day can't make much difference. He wouldn't want you running around in the dark. Please, please come in with me."

"Let me go," Sherri screamed and with an abrupt movement tore away from him and ran off at full speed.

"Damn it, Sherri, come back here!" Barrett implored. He ran after her, his long legs easily shortening the distance between them. He lunged for Sherri's knees and knocked her down into a soft pile of pine needles.

"No, no, no!" Sherri shrieked at him as she clawed at his face and writhed hysterically in his arms.

"Please, Sherri, don't make me hit you," Barrett begged, pinning her to the ground. "I know it's a shock, but get hold of yourself." He stroked her face, but her only answer was to lash clumsily out at him.

"I have to get to my father," she sobbed, her eyes wild and frantic.

Barrett jerked her into a sitting position and drew back his hand to slap her but found that he couldn't. Instead, he wrapped himself around Sherri and held her tightly, letting her flail about at will. The harder she struggled the tighter he crushed her to himself, until she abruptly collapsed against him, and Barrett loosened his hold.

There was a moment of silence, then the still of the black night was broken by her harsh, tearing sobs.

"No one should die without someone's tears to mark their passing," Barrett said with deep sympathy. "You cry all you want, Sherri. You owe your father those tears." His own eyes were full as he thought of the many living relatives he still had and took for granted, while the woman in his arms now had none. Gently he stroked her head, letting her weep, making no effort to end her show of grief.

When at last Sherri was quiet, her head buried in his shoulder, Barrett stood up and swung her easily into his arms. She didn't protest as he carried her back to the cabin, placed her on her bed, and draped a blanket over her shoulders. He then made some coffee and carefully exchanged a cup of it for the sad letter she still held, clutched tightly in her hand.

"Is it okay if I put it on the mantel?" he asked her quietly.

Sherri nodded, her eyes full and brimming. When Barrett had built up the fire once more, he came and sat next to her on the bed. He took the coffee cup, gently removed her boots and socks, then spread her unzipped sleeping bag on the bed and helped her into it. Sherri's hands were like ice, in spite of the warm mug she'd been holding. Barrett removed his own shoes, climbed into the double bag with her and zipped it up. He took her unresisting form into his arms and smoothed her hair away from her face.

"I know this may sound like an impossible suggestion, but try and get some sleep," Barrett counseled. "We'll both get up early tomorrow and find him, okay?"

Sherri nodded, unable to summon even the strength to speak. She swallowed hard, flinching as Barrett reached around her side and pressed a man's linen handkerchief into her hand.

"Thank you, Barrett," she whispered.

"Think nothing of it," was the kind answer. "You cry all you want; it won't bother me at all."

Sherri nodded again, appreciating his kindness. She wondered what would have happened if she'd come up here alone, without Barrett's comforting presence. She would have gone mad, she decided, and she shivered at the thought. Barrett felt the tremor and gathered her even closer. After a long, long time, Sherri felt herself drift off into an unsatisfying sleep. For an even longer time Barrett lay awake, listening to her heavy breathing. And then, tenderly kissing the forehead of the woman beside him, he too closed his eyes and slept.

Sherri moaned in her sleep, tossing her head to escape the nightmares that filled it. She jumped as two hands grabbed her arms, and her eyes fluttered open as she was pulled to a sitting position.

"Wake up, Sherri. It's morning."

Sherri felt awful and wondered why, until the memory of yesterday returned and flooded her consciousness. She blinked and saw that Barrett was already dressed; the horses were saddled and tied out front.

"I'll just be a moment," she said dully, as she grabbed her clothes and headed for the outhouse to change. On her way back she stopped at the pump, where she thrust her face under the cold, running water.

"Are you ready?" asked Barrett, and Sherri felt a rush of gratitude to him. He offered no words or pity, nor asked her such insensitive questions as "How do you feel?" If nothing else, at least the man had tact and understanding.

"Wait a minute." Sherri hurried to the side shed and returned with a sturdy shovel. Eyes downcast, she handed it to Barrett. He took it wordlessly to carry out to the horses. It would be much more useful on the rocky ground than the flimsy folding shovels the rangers were issued.

The horses and their riders fell into their usual positions, with Sherri leading on the mare. The skies were still gray and overcast, and she thought sadly that her father really deserved some sunshine today.

As they neared their destination, Sherri relived the memories of her family's "favorite spot." It was a little hollow, shaded by trees on one side, and open to the sun on the other. The depression was host to many wildflowers, and Sherri's mother had come there often to smell their fragrance while she sewed or read or amused the small child. Her father likened the peacefulness of the area to the gentleness of his wife, who was always happy and contented with her family and her lot in life. Sherri wiped away a tear as they approached the hollow. She reined the horse to a halt, unable to go any further.

Barrett pulled up beside her. "Are we there?"

"It's just over this rise, a small hollow beneath the trees. Just give me a minute, and then we'll go on," Sherri choked out.

"Nonsense." Barrett dismounted and handed Sherri the gelding's reins. "There's no reason for you to subject yourself to this. You stay here and wait. I'll go. Trust me, it'll be easier this way."

"I don't know," Sherri said uncertainly, grateful for his offer but feeling disloyal and cowardly.

Barrett's eyes mirrored her suffering face. "You know your father wouldn't want you to do this if you didn't feel up to it. He said as much in his letter. I think you should remember him as he was, not...this way." He helped her dismount and forced her canteen to her lips.

"You look terrible," he said bluntly. "Sit down, and I'll be as quick as I can."

Barrett reached for the blanket he had brought with him from the cabin.

"Barrett, don't . . . don't hurt him," Sherri stammered. "I mean . . ."

"I'll be real gentle with him," Barrett promised. Impulsively he leaned forward and gave her a quick kiss on the cheek. "Call me if you need me," he told her, then he was gone.

Sherri sat unnaturally still, every second of Barrett's absence ticking away in her head. What if her father wasn't there? What if he *had* survived the winter and lay sick and helpless somewhere, even now calling out for his daughter? Sherri shuddered at the thought, then looked up at the sound of Barrett's approach.

Barrett quickly answered her mute, questioning look with a slow, sad nod that spoke volumes. "He's there, Sherri. I've covered him up." He held out the leather pouch that her father always used to carry. "He had this on him."

Sherri tearfully opened it. Inside was every single one of her letters. She closed the soft leather flap of the bag, then slowly walked toward the hollow. Barrett walked beside her, but as they reached the spot, hung back a little to give her privacy.

Sherri stopped close by the blanketed mound and knelt down. She heard Barrett say, "He was in a very restful position, Sherri. I don't think he suffered at the end." She nodded, grateful for his observation. It seemed so sad that her father had died all alone.

After a time she rose and walked back to Barrett. "My mother is buried a little ways beyond here. We won't need the horses, but we will need the shovel." She strode ahead, through the trees, leaving Barrett to follow.

Barrett began the grim task of digging a grave. The ground was rocky and hard, the high altitude forcing him to gasp for breath. When Sherri tried to relieve him, he angrily waved her back.

"No one should have to dig their own father's grave," was his harsh reply, and Sherri, in her numbed state, could only do as he commanded and sit down again.

Much later, Barrett went into the hollow to carry up the body of Sherri's father. Sherri watched him cradle her father as tenderly as a newborn babe. He carefully laid the blanketed form in the shallow grave, then placed the battered leather hat on top. Barrett straightened up, and again picked up the shovel.

"Why don't you go back to the cabin?" he suggested kindly.

"I'll wait for you," Sherri replied, her voice a monotone.

"For God's sake, go back to the cabin," Barrett urged, and Sherri was shocked out of her numbness to realize that he was waiting until she was out of earshot before he shoveled in the gaping hole. Picking up her father's leather bag, she left without another word and without looking back.

Later, however, while Barrett cleaned up at the pump, Sherri returned to the grave alone. She tied the mare a short distance off, and walked slowly to the site. She gratefully took in the carefully placed stones that formed an even border around the mound of dirt and rocks, and made a mental note to thank Barrett later. He had even transplanted some of the wildflowers so that the grave wouldn't look so bare. Sherri wiped her eyes and tried to think of something to say, some prayer to recite.

Finally she pulled from her pocket the bundle of letters that she had written to her father and set it down among the flowers. She found a flat rock to cover the small stack of worn and faded pages. Straightening up, she took one last look around, no longer bothering to brush away the tears that clouded her vision.

"Goodbye, Dad," she murmured. Then she turned and walked away.

# CHAPTER FIVE

LATER THAT EVENING, Barrett radioed in his daily report. After a quick consultation with Sherri, he also reported her father's death. As Sherri was using her married name and no one, not even Holden, knew her maiden name, the death of an old prospector would not be connected with her. Sherri preferred it that way, and Barrett went along with her wishes.

However, because the proper paperwork would have to be completed at the county registrar's office of births and deaths, Holden asked them to finish out only one week of mapping instead of two. At the end of the week, they were to return to the ranger station.

Sherri didn't know whether to be relieved or not. Staying up at the cabin, surrounded by memories of her father, was painful for her, but at the same time, she dreaded going back to the station—and the curious eyes of her co-workers. The three days she and Barrett had already spent in the high country seemed like years.

Thank goodness for her job. For the rest of that week, Sherri threw herself into it with a dogged determination to work off some of her depression. She and Barrett had achieved an easy, comfortable rapport; while he didn't go out of his way to cater to her every whim, neither did he antagonize her as he had earlier. He talked if she felt like conversation, was quiet if she didn't and went about his business with a professionalism and thoroughness that matched her own.

Sherri was grateful to Barrett for his consideration. By the time they both returned to the station, Sherri had managed to impose some semblance of calm on her turbulent emotions. Outwardly, at least, she was able to appear composed and self-assured to her fellow workers. No one could have guessed from her job performance that anything was wrong.

She and Barrett continued their mutually agreed upon truce, much to the surprise of everyone else. The others were even more amazed to see the two of them taking all their meals together. Only Sherri knew that Barrett had decided upon that course of action by himself. At first, she'd assumed his presence at mealtimes was a mere coincidence, so she deliberately changed her eating schedule. Barrett still showed up. Now, even though Sherri still ate her meals in silence, at least she had company. It was a pleasant change from meals with her previous partners, who had always managed to ruin her appetite with first one complaint, then another.

After a while Sherri became so used to his presence that his absence at breakfast one morning was oddly disturbing. Despite herself, she found her eyes sweeping the room for a sign of him. The tables continued to fill with rangers hungry for breakfast, and to Sherri's dismay, the empty spaces on either side of her were soon occupied. If Barrett did show up, they wouldn't be able to sit together, she thought absently. The realization that she was missing him sank in, and she was immediately annoyed with herself. Her appetite perversely disappeared, and she had decided just to finish her coffee and then leave, when one of the male rangers at the table addressed her.

"Where's your partner?" he asked.

"I have no idea," Sherri replied. "We don't keep tabs on each other."

The man winked at another seated male ranger. "Oh, really?" he continued snidely. "I thought the two of you were inseparable."

Sherri didn't like the unpleasant edge to his voice. "Now just what is that supposed to mean?"

The man gave her a knowing smirk. "It seems to me that the two of you are getting along rather well. You aren't walking around in tears like all his other women partners did, and Barrett hasn't been to Holden's office yelling and screaming for a new partner. I'm just wondering if there's some secret to his success."

Sherri's face flushed as the man's leering smile suggested exactly what he thought had happened to make them compatible working partners.

"I don't think I care for your insinuations," she snapped.

The man shrugged, not at all perturbed by Sherri's anger. "I'm not the only one who's been wondering," he said.

Sherri refused to admit that she had been ordered to get along with Barrett or say goodbye to her job. That was no one's business but hers and Barrett's, and she had no intention of providing these . . . these voyeurs with an explanation.

"I think you're disgusting," she settled for saying instead. Picking up her untouched breakfast tray, she left it on the tray rack and headed for her cabin.

But the subject was not so easily ignored. Sherri's roommate Janet also brought it up. "Sherri, can you two really be getting along that well?" she asked one evening when both women happened to be off duty.

Sherri frowned. "Not really," she answered after considering the question. "It just seems that way, in comparison to all my previous partners."

"Oh." Janet looked disappointed, and Sherri put down her magazine in order to pay closer attention to her friend. "Why do you ask? Come on, what's on your mind?"

Janet sighed. "I was hoping there might be, well, you know . . ." Her voice trailed off.

"Might be what?" Sherri asked, puzzled.

"Might be something going on between the two of you."

She stared at Janet with frank surprise. "There isn't any such thing," Sherri informed her baldly. "Whatever gave you that impression?"

"Nothing, really." Suddenly Janet seemed quite interested in the magazine that Sherri had tossed aside.

"Janet, what's going on? Come on, let's hear it."

"I don't want to say anything that might offend you," Janet warned. But Sherri brushed aside her protests and after much coaxing, Janet agreed to continue.

"The two of you seemed to be getting along so famously that everyone noticed. I've been wondering if maybe you didn't become . . . well, close . . . during your survey trip."

At Sherri's shocked expression, Janet hurried to explain. "I don't mean that the way it sounds. But everyone's been talking, and if there *was* something good happening between you and Barrett, I just wanted to be the first to say how happy I was for you."

There was angry silence from Sherri, and Janet bit her lip. "Now I've gone and done it, haven't I?" she asked in a small voice.

"I cannot believe the nerve of this camp!" Sherri fumed, red patches appearing high on her cheeks. "So now if I'm pleasant to my new partner, it's automatically assumed that I've been charmed into it by his sexual prowess?"

"Sherri, I didn't mean it that way," Janet wailed.

"I can't believe that you of all people would listen to such gossip," Sherri said with bitterness. "I thought that we, at least, were friends. You're as bad as the others," she accused, and Janet flinched. "The most Barrett and I have done is sit together for a few meals! And on the basis of that, the whole camp thinks we're an item?"

Janet ventured timidly, "Barrett seems to like you."

"We are working partners, Janet, that's all!" Sherri insisted. "If you must know, we're only trying to get along so that Holden won't fire us. I hardly see how that can be translated into a torrid love affair!" Here Sherri stopped, too upset to say any more.

Janet tried to repair the damage she had done, but it was too late. Sherri's mixed expression of anger and hurt could not be erased, and Janet left the cabin in tears.

Sherri writhed as she reviewed Janet's words over and over in her mind. The thought of trying to do her job amid crude whispers and sly innuendos distressed her. She almost wished

Janet hadn't told her anything at all, for now she knew that the gossip about her relationship with Barrett was more widespread than she had originally supposed. Tomorrow she would volunteer for another remote assignment, she decided suddenly. She might not be able to stop the rumors, but she could certainly get out of earshot.

The next morning's roll call mustered at dawn for the rangers on the early shift. Holden called out the names to take attendance, then read off the day's open assignments.

"We have a job here: a five-day scouting expedition. Headquarters is worried about the possible fire hazard, and we need new water-level checks for the surrounding sources. Volunteers?"

Sherri raised her hand quickly, so that no one else could beat her to the assignment. "Barrett and I would like the job, sir." She didn't bother to see if Barrett minded her volunteering him without his permission.

"I'd be most pleased to see your report on my desk," Holden declared, nodding his satisfaction. "The rest of you could afford to take a lesson from this young lady on the accuracy of your coordinates."

The rest of the room, however, was busy speculating about the Barrett-Landers team going on another remote assignment so soon after their previous one, and Sherri shifted uncomfortably in her seat.

She couldn't leave the room fast enough to begin packing. Barrett seemed about to follow her, but she successfully eluded him, and for once Barrett decided to leave her alone. He continued to respect her wishes as they left the camp on horseback later that morning.

As usual, Sherri led on the mare, and she set a pace that was hard and driving. Three hours of riding had put a good distance between them and the ranger station, but to Sherri it wasn't enough; she continued to urge the horses on. She had been careful not to converse with Barrett on any subject that wasn't work-related, and her suddenly businesslike demeanor wasn't lost on him.

The horses had just topped a steep rise that flattened out into a grassy area above when Barrett spurred the gelding forward. Drawing alongside the mare, he caught her reins and pulled her to an unexpected halt.

"What do you think you're doing?" Sherri asked indignantly.

Barrett dismounted, then walked up to Ladybug, grabbed Sherri by the waist, and yanked her out of the saddle with such force that she tripped and landed on the seat of her pants.

"Ouch!" she yelped. The water-starved ground was not soft.

Barrett didn't even offer to help her up. Instead he picketed the horses near the grass, then collected both the canteens before returning to Sherri, who still remained sprawled on the ground.

Barrett dropped the canteen beside her with a thump. "You could have at least handed it to me with some politeness," Sherri fumed.

"You're getting as much courtesy from me as I've received from you this morning," was his calm answer. He took a long pull at his canteen, then carefully recapped it.

"Now, partner, I have to admit that you have my curiosity aroused. Whatever small progress we've made in our working relationship, and I do emphasize small—" here Sherri sucked in an angry breath "—seems to have disappeared. This killing pace is the last straw. The horses need a breather, and I am not about to give up my morning coffee break to cater to some ranger with a private bee in her bonnet," Barrett announced forcefully.

He turned his attention to unpacking the coffee pot, a packet of instant, and a small can of butane. "While I'm fixing this, perhaps you could work on becoming a little more human. I don't enjoy riding with robots who speak in one-syllable words."

Sherri jumped to her feet and brushed the dirt off the seat of her jeans. "Don't pretend you don't know why I'm upset," she accused.

Barrett paused. "So there is something wrong. I thought as much." He removed two stacked aluminum cups and deftly separated them. "Do you want to tell me what it is? It might clear the air."

Sherri crossed her arms and clamped her mouth shut. It was bad enough to be the target of malicious rumors, but to have to repeat them was asking too much.

"Just like a woman," Barrett stated. "You expect me to be a mindreader and somehow know exactly what's wrong. Well, it doesn't work that way. You have two choices, Landers. Either you tell me what's bothering you so I can make allowances for your churlish behavior, or you keep your reasons—and your moodiness—to yourself. I expect to be treated with a modicum of civility, if you don't mind."

He was annoyed, of course, but Sherri sensed that there just might be some wounded feelings behind that brusque manner, and she flushed with guilt. She *had* been quite cold to him, unfairly so; deep down, she knew he hadn't been to blame. Barrett was as close-mouthed about his personal business as she was about hers. Even if they had made love, he would have been the last person in camp to advertise it.

"I'm sorry," she apologized. "I just . . ." She stopped, took a deep breath, and started again. "We haven't even been a team for a month yet, and already the whole camp has decided we're an item. First I'm labeled the camp's resident old maid, complete with frigid tendencies, and now I can't wait to get back into the woods to roll around on the ground with you. Talk about going from one extreme to the other. It isn't fair! I just don't understand it!" Her voice rose in anger and confusion, and she couldn't look at Barrett, couldn't meet his eyes.

For a moment, there was silence between them.

"Anyway," she finished, "that's why I volunteered for this remote assignment." Absently, she studied the tips of her boots.

"I suspected that," Barrett sighed.

"I know I should have consulted you," Sherri said apologetically, "but I couldn't stand the dirty comments any longer."

Sherri missed Barrett's eyes fill with sympathy while his mouth compressed into a tight, hard line at the thought of Sherri's ill-treatment by her co-workers.

"It's not as if my reputation in camp is all that great anyway," Sherri went on, unable to keep the disgust from her voice. "But I draw the line at listening to them call me the camp tramp. I hope that you, at least, were spared this nonsense, Barrett."

"Unfortunately, I heard about our rumored affair," Barrett replied honestly.

Sherri's eyes fluttered with dismay. "I'm sorry about that, too," she said, turning away from him on the pretence of checking the horses.

Moments later, two strong capable hands were resting on her stiff shoulders. "Sherri, don't do this to yourself. You may find it hard to put into practice, but you shouldn't let a pack of lies upset you so. Don't let the opinions of people you don't respect have the power to hurt you. To hell with them!" he swore.

Sherri saw the logic of his words and felt slightly mollified. "I suppose you're right," she agreed. "But it makes me so mad! Isn't there anything we can do to stop them?"

Barrett drew her shoulders against his broad chest as he hugged her to him. "Any comments of ours would only have fanned the fire. No one would've believed our denials. The best way to handle this kind of gossip is to ignore it. I did hope that you wouldn't hear about it, though," he said, his voice heavy with regret. "This hasn't been an easy time for you, what with your father's death and all."

Sherri's stiffness began to evaporate as she stood there in his arms. He seemed such a welcome haven, offering such security and strength. And he didn't *have* to do this, she reminded herself. He didn't *have* to be kind to her.

"How did you find out about our rumored affair?" he asked, pleased to feel the tenseness leave Sherri's body.

"Janet congratulated me on the new romance in my life," Sherri reluctantly admitted. "She completely took me by surprise."

"Yes, I'm sure the idea of me as your boyfriend was quite a shock."

Although still locked in his arms, Sherri turned around at the dry irony in voice.

"Landers, I ate all those meals with you so that no would would dare repeat those lies to your face." To Sherri's ears he sounded almost proprietary, but the green eyes were as impassive as ever.

"Oh!" Sherri exclaimed, astounded by his admission. "I never guessed..."

"You wouldn't," was his reply, and Sherri leaped to her own defense.

"I'm sorry, but I never thought of you as the protective type." She carefully studied his face. "Such gallantry is somewhat out of character, isn't it, considering that I'm a big girl who can take care of herself? Not that I don't appreciate the gesture," she was quick to amend.

"Is that a thank you?" Barrett asked sarcastically.

"Please accept my thanks," Sherri said in gracious contrast to her earlier back-handed praise. He deserved that much, at least.

Barrett gently slid a hand under her chin, tipping back her head. "That all depends. My male ego has suffered a terrible blow. Are you saying you want us to be friends?" he asked softly.

"I could certainly use one," Sherri agreed. "And both of us could probably use the practice," she added wryly.

"Truer words were never spoken. Shall we seal the bargain?" He didn't wait for an answer, but lowered his head to join his lips to hers.

Sherri relaxed in his embrace as she wound her arms around his neck. His kiss was exquisitely gentle, with the barest teasing promise of more. Sherri opened her lips, her mouth parting slowly, welcoming a deeper possession. She was not disappointed, for Barrett's lips became more demanding, the kiss more probing as he savored her sweet taste with his tongue.

Sherri closed her eyes and pressed herself closer to the hard, muscled chest. She could feel Barrett's quickened heartbeats reverberating against her own chest, and she lowered her arms from his neck to splay her fingers on his shirt-front. He was so alive, she thought, and all of a sudden, so was she. Those lonely years of her life were suddenly thrust aside, along with all the disappointment and heartache she had known. There was only Barrett and herself, and the aliveness and happiness surging through her veins. And then there was desire.

Sherri's eyes flew open as Barrett's lips traveled to her bare neck. She shivered at the touch, then reciprocated by sliding her hands inside Barrett's shirt and burying her fingers in the curling hair on his chest. Barrett groaned softly and Sherri felt his thigh slip between her jean-clad legs. She reveled in the contact of his aroused body. She was almost in paradise, but not quite, and she wanted more . . .

"Landers, enough!"

Sherri was rudely plummeted back to earth. Barrett pushed her away, and backed off, tucking his shirt back into his jeans. He looked as shaken as Sherri felt.

"Would you stop looking like that," he ordered tersely. Sherri's mouth was half-open, her lips a rosy red from his kisses. Her eyes were glazed with shock and desire, and Barrett knew that he didn't dare look at her again.

"Come on, Landers, we don't want to prove the station rumor-mill right, do we?"

Sherri seemed to snap out of her daze at that. "No. No, I suppose not." She felt hurt and rejected, and a little foolish, too. And something else, something she couldn't quite put her finger on. She was trying to identify it when Barrett's voice intruded into her thoughts.

"I think we should forget about that coffee," he was saying as he repacked the utensils. He frowned at his partner's sudden confusion. "Are you all right?"

Sherri stalled a moment, then plunged ahead. "Just answer me one question, please. Was shielding me from rumors the only reason you joined me for meals?"

"What do you mean?" Barrett's eyes narrowed warily.

Sherri shrugged. "I'm no shrinking violet, Barrett. I can take care of myself—and you know it. So your sudden change of attitude doesn't make any sense."

"Maybe I just wanted the pleasure of your scintillating company."

Sherri laughed heartily. "Oh, really, Barrett. Don't be ridiculous."

Barrett gave her an answering grin. "Friends?" he asked once more as he held out his hand.

Sherri hesitated, then carefully put her own smaller hand in his. "Friends." Her decisive response chased much of the uncertainty from her face, and Barrett was satisfied.

"Let's mount up, partner. We have work to do."

The sun was hot through the thin air of the mountains, and Sherri felt trickles of sweat run down the back of her neck. After an hour's riding, her horse was sweating, too, but fortunately hadn't started to lather. Still, it was time to search for another place to rest.

"See any good places to pull over? The horses are really starting to sweat," Sherri called out.

"They aren't the only ones," Barrett said with disgust. He mopped his brow with a red paisley bandanna. "Lord, it's hot, and we're almost up to the timberline."

Sherri nodded. Holden had good reason to be concerned. One stroke of lightning, one careless camper, could set the slopes ablaze. And the weather had a scorching hotness to it that rarely came to these high altitudes.

Barrett unsaddled the gelding while Sherri did the same for the mare. The horses' backs were soaked under their saddle blankets, and Barrett shook his head.

"I don't like the looks of this at all," he said, his green eyes clouded with worry. "The higher we go, the drier it gets. The woods are one big tinderbox waiting to ignite. We've been riding for hours now, and not one water source we've checked has been at even half its normal level."

"I know." Sherri found a comfortable place on the ground and sat down, taking the opportunity to pull off her heavy boots and socks. "It doesn't look as though we'll have good news for Holden, but it still beats phone duty," she said grinning.

Barrett eased himself down beside her and removed his hat. "You make even this job easy for me," he complimented her. "And so do the horses. Where did you get them?"

Sherri basked in his admiration just briefly before answering. "The state of Colorado has an adopt-a-horse program. The wild mustang herds get too large to support themselves on the limited land preserves. I adopted Ladybug and Brownie while I was still in school. The cost was minimal, and all I had to do was prove that I could provide them with a good home. Many of the Midwest states have similar programs. I'm sure you've heard of them."

Barrett nodded. "I have. But how did you tame them?"

"Well, Dad helped. And they lived up at the cabin in their natural habitat. They quickly caught on that it was nicer to be fed than having to scramble with hundreds of other horses for choice grazing rights. After that, the rest was easy. Dad had plenty of experience with stubborn prospectors' mules, and to him the mustangs were bigger versions of the same animal."

Barrett watched the two horses relaxing in the shade. "What happened to them when you got married?"

"Oh, I took them with me. I couldn't bear to leave them behind, and besides, I never knew how long Dad would be off prospecting. There would be no one to take care of them. They didn't like the city too much," Sherri remembered.

"I can imagine being stabled would be quite a shock after having the run of the country," Barrett said.

"Yes. Thomas didn't like riding, so neither of the horses got much exercise. When he died, I took them, left the city and moved back into the high country. I lived up at the cabin until I was hired as a ranger. You've seen the sad collection of horses the ranger station has. Holden was quite happy when I offered to provide my own mounts."

Sherri shook out her boots and put them back on. "It's nice to see you on Brownie. He hasn't been ridden this much since . . . Dad used to ride him. I was always partial to the mare since she's sweeter-tempered, so the gelding doesn't get out as often as I'd like. Where did you learn to ride?"

"Karen had horses. She taught me." Barrett leaned against a tree trunk, not uncomfortable with the turn the conversation had taken. "I love to ride. While my brothers were out on my father's fishing boats, I'd be out riding. I always wanted to have my own horses, but after the Marines, I moved around too much for that."

He plucked some grass from the ground and threw it in the air. "So how are you doing, Sherri?" he asked, abruptly changing the subject. "I know it hasn't been easy for you since we buried your father."

Sherri leaned back on the same tree trunk and closed her eyes. "I'm doing okay, I guess." There was an uncertain quality in her voice that Barrett recognized.

"And . . . ?" he prompted.

Sherri shrugged. "I don't know if I can explain myself."

"Go ahead and try. The horses need at least another half hour here, so take your time."

Sherri looked over at Barrett. He reclined lazily next to her, but somehow he seemed watchful and alert at the same time.

"Well," she started, "I feel as if a phase of my life has really and truly ended. There's nothing to keep me here anymore. My father is dead, and I have no wish to use the cabin for anything other than a vacation hideaway." Sherri paused to collect her thoughts.

"I have no friends at the station save for you and Janet, and you're only a recent one, at that. I'm tired of being alone. I'm ready for a change, but that's as far as I've taken it."

Barrett stretched out one long leg. "Do you want to find another line of work?"

Sherri laughed ruefully. "I don't know. Even if I did, I have no bankable skills, no college education. But I want to get married again. I want to have children. I want to share the wilderness with them, but not force it on them as the only life to lead. I feel so frustrated sometimes. I'm like a fish out of water in the city. I can't find my way around in a car through rush-hour traffic. Me, the best tracker in the area!"

Sherri shrugged her shoulders in dismay. "I tried to become a part of society when I married Thomas. During those few years, I was starting to find a new niche for myself. I'd like to try it again, somewhere away from here. Away from the people who only know my bad side instead of my good."

"It figures," Barrett said with disgust. "For the first time in three years I find a partner I like and now she wants to leave." His words were mocking, but Sherri thought she detected a trace of sadness in them, too.

"Don't worry," she reassured him. "I don't have enough money to do anything rash. The most ambitious scheme I've concocted is maybe getting myself hired as an advisor for the Girl Scouts."

Barrett turned so that he was now facing her. "What about the gold and silver your father said he left you? Could you do anything with that?"

Sherri laughed aloud at the interested gleam in his eyes. "Miles, that metal couldn't be worth more than a couple of thousand dollars, if that. No, I'll leave it where Dad hid it. Some day, if I have any children, it will be a nice adventure for them to retrieve it."

"That's a relief. I was afraid I'd have to break in a new partner if you hit the motherlode," he said, smiling.

Sherri smiled back. "Dad was good, but this area has been picked clean for decades. Besides, we're not here on a wild-goose chase. We're here to measure water levels."

"Don't remind me," Barrett groaned. "If the horses look at one more empty creek bed today they'll toss us both from sheer frustration."

"We'll find them some water," Sherri told him, "but we won't have any luck just sitting here. I'm ready to go if you are."

Barrett rose, then helped her to her feet. In spite of his fears about the dryness, he admired the view one more time. "It was never like this in the city," he observed.

SHERRI WAS TO REMEMBER those words later, for that afternoon's events had no place in the steel and concrete cities of men. It was after lunch, and Barrett and Sherri were negotiating a trail that ran above a deep ravine. There was no easy way down, and Sherri had decided to stay on the trail and settle for scanning the level of the inside spring from above. She was hot and feeling lazy from her overindulgence of Barrett's cooking, or she would have noticed the faint traces of black smoke showing just over the higher ridge.

"Is that smoke I see?" Barrett called out to her. "Pull up your horse," came his authoritative command as he reached for his binoculars.

Sherri followed the direction of his pointing finger, a sense of dread mixing with self-reproach at her poor attention to the surroundings. The smoke was thin, but it was definitely black.

"I don't smell anything, do you?" Sherri asked as she pulled out her own binoculars.

"No, the wind is blowing the wrong way. Plus that ridge in front of us is blocking the view." Barrett exhaled harshly, his nostrils flaring. "I don't like this at all."

"It can't be that bad," Sherri hoped. "The horses would smell anything before we did, and they don't seem nervous." Sherri tapped her fingers, trying to come to a decision. "Do you think we should try for the top of that ridge and get a better look?"

Barrett glanced sharply at her, then at the ridge. "I don't know. I doubt the horses could handle it. I suggest we radio in the news—"

"I know the procedure," Sherri interrupted, only to be given a black look by Barrett.

"And let the helicopters handle the initial survey," he finished.

"It will take at least an hour or so to get a chopper up here," Sherri argued as she capped her binoculars and put them back in their case. "In the meantime, the station will have no idea of what they're going to be up against."

Barrett shook his head. "I think it's too risky. We don't know how fast that fire is moving. We may end up with flame in our faces when we reach the top of that ridge. There's enough dry vegetation on this side of it to fuel a good-size blaze. I'm guessing the same can be said of the other side. We both know what could happen if we got trapped up here," he reminded starkly, and Sherri shuddered.

"True. Why don't you radio in the coordinates, and we'll let Holden make the decision. That's why he's the one getting the big bucks. Let him—" Sherri abruptly broke off.

"What is it?" Barrett didn't miss the intense look that crossed her face.

"I thought I saw something. A flash, maybe." Sherri was really concerned now. "Not a signal!" she prayed.

"There's no camper registered up here," Barrett said, frowning. "What direction?"

Sherri shaded her eyes as she pointed to a jagged outcropping halfway down the ravine. "There it is again!"

"I saw it." Barrett pulled out his compass and flipped it over to the shiny metal back. He flashed it once, twice, then waited. Within seconds he received two answering flashes.

"Damn it, who could be down there? There aren't any missing-person reports out," Barrett stated as Sherri scrambled to get her own binoculars out of her pack to try to catch a glimpse of the signal's sender.

"I read the bulletin board right before we left. Whoever is down there hasn't been missed by anyone," she answered. "I can't believe this!"

Barrett dismounted, tied the horse, and started to unpack the radio.

"I can't see a thing," Sherri complained. "Even with the infrared, there are too many rock formations and obscure areas."

"I don't like this," Barrett said gloomily. "I'll lay you odds we have injured," he predicted. "And they're right in the path of the fire."

"What kind of fool would rope down into that monstrosity?" Sherri wondered. "Even we haven't had the courage to go down there. Well, Barrett, looks like we'll earn our money today." Sherri dismounted and slung her heavy ropes over her shoulder, then tied the first-aid kit to her belt. "I'm going to try and pinpoint our signaler. Tell Holden we may need that chopper for more than just reconnaissance."

"Will do. Don't you go anywhere without me," he warned her.

"Yes, sir," she mocked. "Your wish is my command." But her face didn't match her careless words.

Sherri kept one eye on the signal's location and the other on her footing. The ground was littered with sharp rocks and loose gravel, a habitual landslide area if she'd ever seen one. If she and Barrett had to climb down into that ravine, she would definitely be wishing she'd packed her hard hat. It took her a good twenty minutes to make her way to the location best suited for descending to the ravine's signaler. She tossed down her ropes and quickly anchored one end of the heaviest rope to a tree, the other end around her waist, before she ventured near the edge. Lying down on her stomach, she was able to see the signaler clearly, even without binoculars. It was a boy! He couldn't be any older than his middle teens.

"Hello down there," Sherri called out, being careful not to dislodge any stones. "I'm from the Colorado Forest Rangers. Can you hear me?"

"Yes," a weak voice called back.

"Are you hurt?" Sherri asked. "How long have you been trapped?"

"I...I don't know. Four days, maybe. I'm just thirsty and hungry, but my brother is hurt."

Sherri felt a sick feeling settle in her stomach, then the familiar surges of adrenaline as she prepared to do the job she was trained for. "How old are you two? What are your names?"

"I'm Rob, and I'm thirteen. My brother is Kevin, and he's fifteen. Are you going to get us out of here?"

"You bet," Sherri answered, using her binoculars to locate the still form of Kevin a couple of hundred feet below his brother, on the very bottom of the ravine. "My name is Sherri, by the way, and I have a partner with me, too, so don't worry. Rob, how badly is your brother hurt? Is he still talking?"

Rob mumbled something indistinct, and Sherri had to ask him to speak up.

"He was until this morning. He said he thought he broke his leg. I . . . you don't think he's dead, do you?" The boy's voice rose on a sob, and Sherri hastened to reassure him.

"I think he just passed out from the pain, Rob. We'll take care of him. Now listen to me. I need to know your last name, and I need to know if anyone is looking for you. What about your parents?" Sherri asked as she tied her canteen to a thinner utility line and slowly began to lower it to the boy.

"Our name is Walker. Kevin and I were supposed to go to summer camp, but we got off the bus early. My father is away on a business trip, and my mother is with Grandma right now."

"No one is looking for you?" Sherri asked with disbelief.

"Kevin didn't think so," Rob answered, and then asked "Is this for me?" as the canteen reached him.

"Yes, it's water. Take little sips of it, nice and slow, Rob, or else it might all just come right back up."

"I'll save some for Kevin. He was really thirsty. He doesn't have much shade," came the sobbing words.

"Don't you worry, Rob. We've already radioed for a helicopter, and we'll get down to Kevin as soon as we can. I'm going to talk to my partner, then I'll be right back to see about getting you out of there."

Sherri edged away from the yawning space and stood up.

"Mobile to base, mobile to base," she radioed on the walkie-talkie.

"Come in, mobile, this is base. Over?"

"It doesn't look good, partner," Sherri said as she filled Barrett in on the situation.

Barrett muttered a four-letter expletive that made her flinch. "Sherri, the smoke is getting worse. I don't know if you can see it with all those overhangs above you, but both the horses and I can smell it now. Do you think we could evacuate the boys with a chopper?"

"Negative, base, negative. The reverberations from the rotor would send rocks crashing down all over the place. We'll have to get them out ourselves. Do you think we can wait until the chopper brings proper rescue gear? Barrett, all we have is a few ropes for emergencies! We packed for a survey expedition, not a major rescue!"

For a moment there was only static over the radio, then Barrett's strong voice came booming through. "Those kids will be dead before then. There's another fire on the northeast rim, and all the choppers are over there dropping water. Who knows when they'll get here."

"All right. All right." Sherri stopped to consider her options. "It will take you about twenty minutes to hike over here. Can you see me?" She waved her arms in an exaggerated gesture.

"Now I can. Over."

"I'm going to climb on down to the first boy. He's only about a hundred feet or so down and isn't injured. I'll secure him with the ropes, and he should be ready for you to haul up when you get here. You can take him back to the horses. The fire won't feed on your bare side of the ravine and he'll be safe. By the time you come back I'll be down to the other boy. Agreed?"

"I hate it," Barrett protested.

"I'm not crazy about it, either, but you're too heavy for me to haul out of the ravine, so I'm the logical choice to climb down. Look, Barrett, bring every rope you've got. We're going to need them. Over."

"Isn't there any way we can get the horses in there to help with the hauling?" Barrett asked, hoping against hope. Even with his iron nerves, he couldn't help cringing at the black smoke growing steadily closer.

"Negative, base. Let's get going. Out." Sherri shut off her radio, taking a few seconds to pause, to steel herself for the grueling task ahead. Across the ravine she saw Barrett give her a wave, and she smiled. Thank goodness Holden hadn't given her the woman partner she'd originally requested but a great big bear of a man instead. They just might make it yet.

Sherri was an experienced climber and rapeller, but even the best of climbers would have been nervous descending with no equipment except a single rope. The drop was steep, offering just enough footholds to keep Sherri's gloved hands from sliding down the rope at an out-of-control speed. She breathed a sigh of relief when she reached the jagged outcrop of rock that was the young boy's position.

"Would you like a drink?" Rob asked gallantly. Without the white, scared face he would have been an engaging youngster.

"Thanks, maybe later," Sherri said as she untied herself and sat down beside him. "How're you doing, sport?" she asked, opening her first-aid kit. "Do you hurt anywhere?"

"Not really. You don't look like a park ranger. Where's your uniform?" Rob asked.

Sherri gently cleaned and covered the boy's numerous scrapes and abrasions. "I'm not a park ranger, I'm a forest ranger. There's a difference. And we don't always wear uniforms." She checked his limbs for broken bones. "Does this hurt?"

Rob shook his head. "I'm fine. What about Kevin?"

"I radioed my partner, and he's on his way. He'll haul you up first, and then he'll lower me down to get Kevin."

Rob looked fearful. "Kevin and I fell doing that. I didn't want to, but Kevin said it would be fun. Weren't you . . . won't you be scared?" He swallowed noisily.

"We do this all the time," Sherri reassured him. "A little fear can be healthy. It keeps me on my toes. And my partner is fearless. He's an ex-Marine, rough and tough."

"Hey, my uncle is a Marine! They eat nails, my dad says." Rob's face brightened. "What's his name?"

"Barrett," Sherri answered as she began to knot a harness around the boy with the extra ropes she carried.

"I wonder if my uncle knows him," Rob mused, and Sherri was relieved to see that the boy's mind was still functioning clearly.

"Landers, you down there?" came a hail from above.

"That's him," Sherri informed Rob, delighted to see a smile break out on the boy's face. "You and your brother are halfway home now."

"I have the boy all ready," Sherri called out. "Start pulling on my command. Let me help you stand up, Rob, and then I'll show you what we're going to do."

She never had that chance. Rob lurched to his feet and instantly fainted from fear and lack of food. Sherri caught him, and decided it was probably just as well that he would be spared any awareness of the ordeal.

"What's the delay?" Barrett shouted down.

"The poor kid has fainted," Sherri called back.

"He doesn't look too heavy," Barrett said. "I shouldn't have any problems." Carefully, with Sherri at first supporting the limp body, Barrett hauled the child up, hand-over-hand, until he was able to grab Rob and lift him over the edge onto level ground.

"Is he okay?" Sherri called, her eyes shielded from the sun as she looked up.

"He's still out of it, but he seems okay," Barrett answered. He glanced at the sky and then at his watch.

"It will take me at least half an hour to get to the horses and then the usual twenty minutes to get back to you. How about if I lower you down before I go? Rob should be okay up here for a few more minutes, and it would save time if you could finish attending to the other boy before I get back."

"I can smell that smoke now, Barrett," Sherri said nervously, recognizing the validity of his suggestion. "Sounds good to me."

Barrett took his longer rope and knotted it to Sherri's, which he had removed from the unconscious boy. "It's at least twice the distance down as it was pulling Rob up," Barrett shouted.

"Forget the measurements and throw me the makeshift harness," Sherri responded for she was uneasy and in a hurry to get started.

"Stand clear," Barrett called before tossing down the lengthened rope.

Sherri caught it, and then the harness. She loosened the harness to fit herself, then secured it to the rope and slipped it on. She noticed Barrett above her crossing himself in what looked like a religious gesture.

"Is that for me or for you?" she called out as she signaled her readiness.

"Both of us," was the terse answer. "Ready?"

"Ready," she replied. The rope dug into her chest, but Sherri welcomed its firmness as she half climbed, half floated down the steep side of the ravine. Her ribs ached in protest, but she could not complain, knowing that there was an injured or even dead boy below her. Those children should be grounded the rest of their lives, she thought angrily. And the parents should be jailed for having raised such irresponsible children. *Please don't let that young boy be dead,* she prayed, *and please don't let Barrett get tired and drop me. He must be strained to the breaking point by now.* She stopped and carefully planted herself in one of the few footholds, to afford both Barrett and herself a short rest.

"I know you have your radio on, but you don't have to answer. I just wanted to give you a breather," Sherri said into her walkie-talkie. She wasn't able to see the man above her breathe a sigh of relief or see his hands clench the rope even tighter than before.

She twisted slightly and looked below her, happy to observe that they were more than halfway to the bottom. "Barrett, only about another hundred feet to go. Hang on, partner, we're almost there. Give me ten seconds, then start lowering me again," she radioed. She fastened the radio to her belt and grabbed the rope. She began to move again, slowly, steadily descending, until her feet touched rocky but level ground.

She untied the rope, then rushed over to the motionless form of Rob's brother. He was unconscious and in shock—but alive.

"Hey, baby doll, are you okay? Over!" came the concerned question, phrased in non-regulation words.

Sherri waved and fumbled for her walkie-talkie again, amazed at how badly her hands were shaking. "This is baby doll, sweetcakes," she teased, her voice trembling and hoarse. "He's still alive, Barrett. Get going."

"Right. Over and out."

Sherri thanked her lucky stars that she had finally been teamed with a partner who didn't obstruct her with interminable questions. Right now, time was of the essence, and one look at the blackness of the sky behind her was testimony to that. The smell of smoke was getting more acrid by the minute. Sherri prayed that Barrett had tied the horses securely; if the helicopters couldn't see to land, she and Barrett would have to evacuate the children by horse.

Sherri splinted Kevin's broken leg with the ease of long experience. She suspected broken ribs and possibly a sprained wrist from the fall. She hoped there were no spinal injuries, because a move by rope would certainly aggravate them, but they had no other choice. Both the sloping side she had descended and the bottom of the ravine itself were full of vegetation, and the fire could catch as easily there as anyplace else.

She checked her watch. Another few minutes and Barrett should be back. "Hurry up, Barrett," she said aloud, and as though he'd heard her, his voice came crackling over the radio.

"Base to mobile, base to mobile. Sherri, are you there?"

"Yes. Barrett, have you checked with Holden? What's the E.T.A. on that chopper?"

"Not good. I wish we could basket him out with one, but even if we chanced sliding the rocks, it's a no go. We won't get a chopper for another hour yet, and those flames are so close I can hear them."

Sherri's heart sank. "That close?" she repeated, hoping she had heard wrong.

"Sorry, partner. It's just you and me."

"And one beat-up kid. He's all ready for you, Barrett. You can haul when you're ready. Just take it easy. Fifteen is too young to live in a wheelchair."

"How much would you say he weighs?" Barrett asked.

"He looks pretty thin. But he's easily over a hundred pounds, maybe a hundred and twenty. Can you handle him Barrett?" Sherri asked anxiously.

"Considering you weigh close to that yourself, Landers, you sure as hell had better hope so," he replied with meaningful emphasis, and Sherri's palms started to sweat as the inert form of Kevin began to rise slowly up the ravine.

Sherri did some mental calculations. Barrett had lifted Rob out, then lowered her in. Now he was lifting Kevin out. The man was strong, but brute force couldn't last forever especially without proper equipment. She saw Kevin's progress becoming slower and slower. There was no way at all that Barrett could pull her up, too, not after having carried first one boy, and now having to carry another, on a twenty-minute hike to safety. Not unless he took the time to rest between exertions, and time was something they didn't have.

Sherri's stomach fluttered. She would have to find her own way out, and knowing Barrett, he wasn't going to agree. She closed her eyes tightly, then made up her mind. As soon as Kevin was safe, she would make certain Barrett didn't risk his safety for hers. All her life, Sherri's father had taught her to take care of herself, and she would. Even if it scared her silly, she thought.

Kevin finally reached the top. "Barrett, are you okay?" Sherri radioed.

His voice was hoarse and she could hear his labored breathing. "Yeah," he gasped out.

"Good, now toss down my end again," Sherri commanded. When Barrett had, she asked, "How's Kevin?"

"The boy's still breathing, but he looks awful."

"Better get him out of that harness. He'll probably breathe better," Sherri suggested with calm purpose. "Let me know when he's clear."

"He's clear," Barrett called back a few minutes later.

"Are you?" Sherri asked innocently.

"Yes, but why..."

Sherri wasn't listening. She gave the rope a mighty tug, and then scurried out of the way as it came falling the almost three hundred feet down.

Barrett's roar of frustration could be heard without benefit of a radio. His stream of curses was loud and voluble, and although she was far away from him, Sherri still shivered at his fury. When his voice finally sounded on the radio, it was deadly quiet.

"Exactly what are you trying to do, partner?" The voice whiplashed on the last word, and Sherri almost didn't pick up her radio.

"I'm being noble, what do you think?" she finally snapped.

"Do you think you're going to sprout wings all of a sudden, you stupid little fool?" Barrett shouted, and Sherri lowered the volume on her radio to compensate for his excessive loudness.

"The fire will reach the ridge before you get back. You don't have wings either," she said with irony. "In any event, you're too tired right now to haul me up. I wouldn't even trust you with my canteen at the end of the rope," Sherri declared.

"You'd better keep that canteen, Landers, because you're going to need it when it starts getting hot." His voice broke on the last word, and Sherri felt a sudden stab of pity for him. She knew how helpless he must feel.

"I'll be fine, Barrett. I'm going to try and climb out over that landslide area. There're a lot of handholds."

Barrett took a few minutes to get control of his voice, then switched on the radio again. "Sherri, that way out leads to the area closest to the ridge. You'll be going from the frying pan into the fire, literally!"

"You can't risk the boy's life by pulling me up now, even if you had the strength. The fire is moving too fast. I'll have more time if I hike around the ravine and over to your side than if I waited for you to get back. I'll make it," she said with feigned confidence.

"You won't. You'll end up under a pile of rocks," he predicted bitterly.

"Thanks for the confidence, partner," Sherri spat out. "Why don't you just shoot me before the flames come and save me from a fate worse than death?"

Sherri heard his sharp intake of breath, and she instantly regretted her hasty words, knowing without seeing him that his face must be gray with worry.

"I didn't mean that," she apologized. "Look, there's no other way. You get Kevin out of there, then wait for me on the other side, okay? I may need a helping hand."

"Please be careful, Sherri," he pleaded. "I'm not up to breaking in a new partner."

"Roger, partner. I promise you won't have to if I can help it." Sherri's face was grim. "Wish me luck," she said, depressing the transmit button for the last time.

Barrett crossed his fingers, then uncrossed them as he prepared to lift Kevin and make his way back to the horses and safety.

Sherri gathered up the rope and neatly wound it into a coil that fit over her shoulder and across her chest. One cardinal rule was never to leave equipment behind. You didn't know if you'd need it later. Sherri quickly gathered up the harness and fastened it to her belt. She stood still for a minute, trying to decide on the safest course.

It was impossible to climb up the sheer side of the ravine. Unfortunately, that was where Barrett and the horses would be. She'd have to climb up the less steep, more vegetated side and walk around the end of the ravine to double back, but there was no alternative. Provided those rocks didn't start shifting, she'd be able to make it. If the fire didn't cut her off, a nagging little voice told her.

Sherri started up the ravine toward the rock-slide area. She gingerly tried her footing and decided that as long as she was slow and careful, she shouldn't have any major problems. She pushed the coil of rope onto her back, then tossed her long braid over her shoulder. Here goes, she thought.

Barrett watched her progress as he struggled to carry the injured boy back to the horses. He was so tired. Sherri had been right; he wouldn't have had the strength to haul her out, but he didn't enjoy the helpless feeling that overwhelmed him and filled him with sick fear. He could see her, a tiny figure making intolerably slow progress over the gigantic pile of loose rocks. Barrett checked on the boy within his arms, then again fastened his eyes on the woman far below.

He hated the nauseous, sweating terror, hated the feeling of being in a nightmare that was never going to end. It had been bad enough when he was lowering her on the rope, but then he'd been distracted by his concentration on the grueling task of controlling her descent. Now he could do nothing but watch her, and the agony of suspense was doing more to undermine his strength than his physical labor had earlier. To think she'd yanked her lifeline right out of his hands! He didn't need her courage, he told himself, anger at her actions again overwhelming him. When Sherri got herself out of this he was going to give her a piece of his mind! If she got herself out ... He forced his aching muscles to speed up, moving as quickly as his burden and the loose ground would allow.

A shower of rocks clattered downward under Sherri's feet, and she started to lose ground and slip. Every time she tried to speed up her progress, the same thing happened. She could go only so fast and no faster. Sherri wished she could see the advance of the fire, but she could hear it and see the bits of black floating in the breeze. The air had begun to heat up, and Sherri wiped her wet brow. She was only halfway there.

Turning sideways, she noticed that Barrett had reached the horses and was following her progress. He gave her a wave of encouragement, and Sherri felt renewed strength flood through her. She again began her assault, but by the time she was three-fourths of the way up, the fire had spread to the top of the ridge and was moving down the sloping side toward the ravine.

Sherri willed her muscles to continue their slow, steady motion of ascent. The urge to hurry was strong, but yielding to it would be unwise. She'd lose more ground than she'd gain. In the distance, one of the horses screamed in fear at the approaching flames and the sound seemed to echo the scream in Sherri's head.

"Come on, Landers, you're almost there," Barrett urged aloud as he finished blanketing Kevin. He grabbed an extra blanket to bring with him, then bolted for the opposite side of the ravine, racing as fast as he could.

The last few feet of rock passed under Sherri's hands, and suddenly she was up and over the edge. She dragged herself a little farther forward, then lay on the ground, gasping for air. The flames were only minutes away, and the air was hot and scorching. Sherri forced herself to rise and begin crawling on her hands and knees, the air cooler and more breathable near the ground.

A small arrow of fire had already reached the ravine. Barrett could dimly see her on the ground through the flames,. "Move it, Sherri, move it, or you'll be trapped!" he called out frantically.

Sherri's oxygen-starved brain barely registered his words, but it did recognize their urgency. Rising to her feet, she stumbled toward the sound of his voice.

"Run, baby, run!" Barrett yelled at the top of his voice, the cords of his neck taut with the effort.

Run Sherri did. She ran straight toward the partially obscured figure of her partner. The fire cut her off from him, but so far it was only waist-high. Gathering her speed for a jump, she lengthened her stride and ran like she had never run before.

Barrett was almost in the flames himself, watching the wild-eyed woman from the other side with eyes as raging as hers. His teeth closed on his lip as she jumped, then broke through the skin as he saw her effort fail. The rescue, coupled with her climb in the oxygen-poor atmosphere, had taken its toll. Sherri's body flew through the flames, and within seconds she was on clear ground, her clothes and hair afire.

Barrett was on her instantly with his blanket, smothering the flames and frantically rolling her in the dirt. The heat, the shock and the airless tent under the blanket were more than Sherri's strangled lungs could take. With a gasping sigh, she closed her eyes. Her last memory before the world slipped away from her was Barrett's anxious voice.

"Did you have to bring the damn rope, too?"

# CHAPTER SIX

IT SEEMED ONLY MINUTES ago to Sherri that she'd closed her eyes, but when she opened them again to see the white walls of the first-aid station around her, she knew she must have been mistaken. She felt a weight on her face and automatically tried to brush off the foreign object with her hands. Agonizing, unbearable pain shot through her fingers, and Sherri screamed, or rather, she tried to. Her hoarse, heat-scorched throat could only emit a croak, which alerted the nurse in the room.

"Hi, Sherri. Do you remember me? Just nod, don't try to talk," cautioned Arlene, the station's resident nurse.

Sherri nodded.

"Good. Do you remember what happened?"

Sherri nodded a second time. "The boys..." she croaked.

"They're in the next room. The three of you will be flown to Denver as soon as the helicopter that brought you here has refueled. It was pretty low when it picked you up from the ravine."

Sherri could have screamed again, but this time from frustration. She didn't care about fuel levels, for heaven's sake. Where was Barrett? He would let her know what had happened.

"Want Barrett," she whispered as loudly as she could, trying to talk through the oxygen mask that was covering her mouth and nose. "Take this off," she added, her throat burning with the effort.

Arlene complied. "Just for minute to see if you can breathe all right without it," she qualified. "Your partner is outside, but I don't know..."

Sherri kicked the side of the bed rail with her boot. Then she kicked it again, emphasizing her need.

"Okay, okay! I'll send him in, but only if you promise not to talk."

Sherri nodded her head once, observing that her face hurt too, but not nearly as much as her bandaged hands.

Like her, Barrett was still dressed in his dirty clothes. Sherri was pleased to note that he looked uninjured. She started to speak, but Barrett held up his hand. "You have a burned throat from breathing the hot air," he warned. "I'll talk, you nod, and I think I can anticipate most of your questions, okay?"

Sherri gave a slight nod "Yes."

Barrett ran his hands through his hair, then dragged a chair close to her bed and sat down. There was no grace in his motions now, and he sank like a rock thrown into water.

"First of all, how are you feeling? Much pain?"

Sherri shrugged. There wasn't, really, if she kept her arms still.

"You've already had a shot of morphine. Arlene radioed the doctor, and he okayed it. You were out for about two and a half hours, I'd say. You've been here at the camp for over an hour, and you and the boys are being flown to Denver's Lutheran Hospital in about twenty minutes."

Sherri looked down at her hands, then back at him. Barrett's jaw tightened. "Let me backtrack a bit, then I'll get to your injuries."

Sherri rolled her eyes in frustration, careful to avoid any jarring movement of her head. She suddenly realized that she was thirsty. "Drink?" she croaked out.

"No, the doctor said not yet. Are you going to listen to me or not?" he asked, half-rising as if he were going to leave.

Sherri nodded vigorously, then immediately closed her eyes as her head and face started to ache. There was an odd, burnt smell in the air, and she sniffed inquiringly. Was that coming from her?

Barrett noticed her actions and sighed. "Have it your way, Landers. About your hands," he began slowly. "They're in pretty bad shape. They're covered with third-degree burns, and you're going to need surgery. That's why you can't have anything to drink. Once you get to Denver, you'll be taken straight to the operating room. The rest of you isn't too bad, mostly second-degree burns, and a few places where your clothing melted into your skin. They'll undress you under anesthetic later, I'm guessing. There are some patchy spots on your legs, and a lot of blistering on your face.''

Barrett watched her carefully for signs of hysteria, but all he saw was clear eyes waiting calmly for the rest of the facts, and he continued. ''That awful smell is your hair. It caught fire, too, and the melted mass hasn't been trimmed away yet, on account of your face being burnt. Your face doesn't seem much worse than a bad sunburn to me, but the nurse wanted to let the doctor see you first. It isn't bad enough to be bandaged like your legs or hands.''

Sherri lifted her hands to touch her hair but gasped at the effort and froze in mid-movement.

Barrett gently lowered her hands back onto the pillows at her sides. ''For heaven's sake, don't do that,'' he warned, his green eyes cloudy.

Sherri silently agreed. She opened her mouth, then decided against talking and raised her foot to point toward the mirror above the sink. Barrett grasped her meaning instantly.

''Forget it. You look like hell, take my word for it,'' he told her bluntly.

She lowered her leg again, noting that the upper thigh was bandaged right over the fabric of her pants, but it didn't seem to hurt nearly as badly as her hands.

Sherri's eyes flew to Barrett's. ''What else?'' she tried to say with them.

Barrett lightly touched her uninjured shoulder with his large hand. ''The helicopter came shortly after I carried you over to the boys. The fire's under control now, by the way, but it could break out again at any time. The chopper flew the four of us to the station and— Don't worry, I sent someone back for the horses," he said quickly in response to her worried look. "They should be on their way home by now," he assured her.

"The boys are doing fine. Arlene seems to think that Kevin will pull through even though he's still unconscious. Janet's packing a bag for you for the hospital, and she promises to take good care of the horses while you're gone."

"How long?" Sherri whispered. A few weeks, maybe? A month?

Barrett didn't answer right away. Sherri kicked the bed rail again, and he looked up.

"I don't know; I'm not a doctor. Probably not long," he said offhandedly, and Sherri closed her eyes in relief. She had never been in a hospital in her life, but she was certain she wasn't going to enjoy it. Who ever did?

But wait, why couldn't Barrett take care of the horses for her? She frowned, knowing that Janet didn't like to ride and fearing they wouldn't get enough exercise. Barrett noticed her frown.

"Now what? I thought I covered everything," he said, trying to mask his pity and concern for her.

"Not Janet, you," Sherri whispered before breaking into a dry, painful cough.

"Me? What do you . . . oh, the horses!" he said with sudden understanding. "I won't be here to take care of them. I'll be going with you."

Sherri felt both relief and surprise at this announcement. Relief that she wouldn't be going into hospital in a strange city alone, but surprise that he would be allowed to go with her. It was most irregular. Policy restricted rangers from accompanying injured partners unless they were related, and policy didn't allow relatives to serve at the same ranger station in the first place. Barrett was disliked, true, but not enough for Holden to permit him to leave the station, especially with every ranger needed because of the continuing fire hazard.

Sherri was suddenly too tired to talk anymore. Her hands started to throb in earnest, and she shivered and closed her eyes. Barrett drew the blanket up gently.

"It must hurt," he said compassionately. "I'll call the nurse. Maybe she can give you something else for the pain."

She opened her eyes to catch him staring at her hands with a strange expression. Instantly the old impassiveness settled back into place, but Sherri wasn't fooled. She looked down at her hands, then back at him, questioning his concern.

After a moment, Barrett said, "You don't play the piano, do you? Or the guitar, maybe?"

Sherri shook her head slightly; it seemed to take great effort.

"Well, then, you have nothing to worry about," he said briskly. "You'll be abusing your horses with your reins in no time." He grinned wickedly.

Sherri tried to glare daggers at him, but she could only grin weakly back. She winked one eye to let him know she was on to his game. Then it seemed easier just to close both of them and rest.

Arlene entered the room, and from a hazy distance Sherri heard her say, "Well, Barrett, we're ready to get you and your fiancée onto the helicopter. Would you see if her roommate's finished packing her bag?"

*Fiancée?* That wasn't right, Sherri mumbled to herself, eyes still closed. That Barrett—no wonder Holden was letting him accompany her. The man had his nerve, she thought dreamily. Still, she would be glad of Barrett's presence, whatever his motives for the lie.

"You be careful with her," Barrett warned Arlene. Sherri almost started at the sharpness of his voice. She thought she felt something gently brush against the cracking skin of her cheek, but she wasn't sure, because she was sinking quickly into the oblivion of drug-induced sleep.

SHERRI WAS NEVER ABLE to recall much of what happened during the following weeks. When she wasn't in a drug-induced haze following repeated skin grafts to her hands, she was heavily sedated for continual bandage changes and whirlpool therapy to slough away dead tissue. Sherri was amazed that her two small hands could cause her so much agony, and she finally stopped fighting the drugs, allowing herself to drift away to a blurry, surreal world that was removed from pain.

Eventually, however, her hands healed enough that the narcotic pain-killers were no longer needed. Gradually Sherri became more and more aware of her surroundings and stayed awake for longer periods of time. The first person who noticed her improved faculties was Barrett.

The day was cold and rainy; the welcome moisture pelted in large drops against the window. This was no warm summer shower, but a harsh, blustery autumn gale shrouding the area in bleak shades of gray. It was the sound of the rain against her window that Sherri heard, the sound of the rain that slowly drew her mind out of the silent fog it had wandered in for so long.

She opened her eyes and kept them open, although she couldn't focus properly at first. But the sound of falling rain had always been soothing to Sherri, even as a child, and she lay contentedly still in her bed. After a while her eyes cleared, and she let them sweep curiously around the room. They widened at the sight of the man seated across from her. His attention was on the rainy scene outside the darkened window, and in the gloom he didn't notice Sherri's scrutiny at first.

The faint afternoon light threw his face into sharp relief. It was thinner, the facial planes harsher than Sherri remembered. Barrett's hair was longer, too, with an untidy shagginess that Holden certainly would have disapproved of. His clothes were casual: jeans and a long-sleeved shirt worn as a concession to the rain. His chin rested on one updrawn knee, and Sherri wondered how much time he had spent in her room posed just like this. Calm, controlled, comforting—yes, *comforting*; that was the word that sprang to Sherri's mind. His presence was like the falling rain, soothing, and all enveloping.

Barrett turned his head and discovered her watching him. "Hi, there, sleepyhead," he said quietly as he dropped his leg, easily adjusting his body to face her bed.

"How are you?" Barrett's voice was soft, not urging immediate conversation.

"Fine." Sherri's answer came out just as softly, but without a trace of her former hoarseness.

"Do you want me to call a nurse for your pain meds?" Barrett was anticipating her answer, and quickly reached for the call bell.

"No, I don't . . ." Sherri paused and blinked, trying to clear her mind. "No," she settled for saying.

"Oh." Barrett replaced the button, looking first surprised, then pleased. "In that case, what would you like?"

"To stay awake," was her prompt answer. She felt like Sleeping Beauty, awakening from a hundred years' sleep.

"Would you sit me up and talk to me?"

Barrett smiled then, his lips parting in a grin of pure delight as he gently complied with her wishes. He elevated the head of the bed and deftly rearranged her pillows.

"Well, well, Landers," he said with satisfaction. "Welcome back to the land of the living."

Sherri could think of nothing to say, for that smile transformed his rugged facial features into breathtaking attractiveness. Never before had she thought of Barrett as handsome.

"I'm glad you're here," she said shyly. She vaguely remembered that he had been with her most of the time during her stay. She couldn't remember the events, but she could place the memory of his presence. Something else nagged at her; she tried to concentrate, tried to sweep the cobwebs from her brain. She frowned, and Barrett was suddenly alert.

"Are you in pain?" he asked, his face losing the attractive glow.

"It's not that." Sherri looked up at him, studying his green eyes. "But I feel so frustrated! I can't seem to remember things right." She started to turn her hands palms up in an instinctive gesture of despair but caught herself in time. Then, curious, she carefully lifted the two bandaged mounds and brought them onto her lap for inspection.

"Don't force it," Barrett cautioned. "How do they feel?" he asked, motioning with one graceful hand to her covered ones.

Sherri tentatively moved her wrists. "Sore, but not unbearably so. How do they look?"

"Better than when you first arrived," Barrett answered promptly. "I didn't get to see too much of them, though, during your treatments. You were in too much pain. I usually ended up being thrown out of the room while they sedated you." Barrett's face was rigid with the memory, and Sherri blushed in embarrassment.

"I'm sorry," she murmured lamely. "I . . . I don't remember."

"Don't apologize," Barrett said curtly. "You have no reason to be sorry. And if I were you, I wouldn't be so eager to remember these past few weeks, either. Your body went through things that nightmares are made of. Be glad your mind escaped untouched."

"Oh." Sherri was suddenly uncomfortable, and she shifted in her bed. Had she made a fool of herself during her illness? She honestly couldn't remember very much, other than the agonizing pain in her hands and her desire to escape it.

The two of them listened to the rain for a while, then Barrett broke the uncomfortable silence. "Now I've upset you. I didn't mean to." It was his turn to apologize. "But trust me, you're better off not remembering. You're very lucky. There's no need to relive the pain." He shook his head. "I never thought I'd end up rescuing my injured partner. Especially not Sherri Landers, the station's pride and joy," he gently mocked. "Well, enough of that," he said briskly, dismissing the memories as too painful for Sherri to dwell on.

"Not an injured partner. An injured baby doll," she said, smiling.

Barrett again shook his head, but this time in confusion. "Huh?"

"You called me a baby doll. Over the walkie-talkie. Don't you remember?"

"No, I don't." Barrett stiffened, his dignity under fire.

"You did!" Sherri insisted.

"I am not responsible for anything I said under stressful conditions." Barrett crossed his arms defensively across his broad chest.

"There was something else..." Sherri screwed up her face in concentration and realized that it didn't hurt at all. If she could have seen herself, she would have noticed only a few patchy, scaling areas. They were all that remained of the burns on her face.

"There wasn't anything else. Can I get you something to drink?" Barrett asked, trying to change the subject. "How about a mirror? Would you like to see your new hairstyle? One of the nurses gave you a new cut. Your hair isn't as long as it was before, but it looks nice."

A mirror! Barrett's suggestion brought back that awful afternoon in the ranger station as she waited for the helicopter. She had demanded a mirror, and Barrett had refused.

"You said I looked terrible!" Sherri accused, memory flooding back in a rush of certainly. "And you said we were engaged!"

"Flattery, my dear, but thank you anyway. I think your memory is still a little fuzzy." His voice had lost its gentle tones, and the old, insufferable Barrett of the ranger station was back—but Sherri knew she was right.

"I may not remember the time I've been here very well, but I remember the ranger station. You said I was engaged to you! That's why Holden let you stay here. It has to be. Otherwise, you'd be off digging firebreaks. You don't have so much seniority or vacation time that you can afford to spend it all sitting around in Denver." Sherri paused to catch her breath. Lord, she felt weak. She wasn't up to any verbal sparring. And she had another question, too.

"Just how long have I been here?" she asked unsteadily, leaning back against the pillows.

"Over two weeks, almost three," Barrett answered as he reached for the nurse's call button.

"Three weeks, but— Barrett, don't do that!" Sherri insisted when she saw him pick up the button. "I want to talk to you!" She exhaled sharply as he ignored her wishes. "Barrett, why—"

"Not now. You're getting too upset," he broke in, "and I'm sure your doctor will want to know that you're back with us."

"Why? What's going on? What's been happening to me?" Sherri's voice was weak, and suddenly she felt weepy and shaken, but she refused to prove Barrett right by crying.

Barrett leaned over and gently covered her forearm with his hand. "You've been sick, that's all. It's all the drugs. You'll feel better once you get them out of your system."

Sherri nodded, but she couldn't stop a tear from trickling out of the corner of a closed eye. Barrett noticed it, and his face became grim.

"Sherri, please! If you cry, they might not let me visit you this evening! We won't be able to finish our conversation. I promise to answer all your questions," he wheedled in an attempt to cheer her up.

Sherri opened her eyes. "All of them?"

Barrett kissed her nose, then wiped her eyes with a tissue from her nightstand. "Well, most of them," he hedged.

He laid a consoling hand on her shoulder, and Sherri leaned against him, drawing strength from his nearness. Moments later, the nurse found them still in that position.

"Look who's back with us," Barrett said proudly, gesturing toward Sherri's bright, alert eyes and smiling face.

"Why, Miss Landers!" The nurse proceeded to take her vital signs and ask her some questions, then she shooed Barrett out of the room.

"You'll have to leave now, Mr. Barrett. I'm going to call the doctor, and I'm sure he'll want privacy to examine Sherri."

Barrett nodded, heading for the door, and Sherri panicked. "You'll wait outside for me, won't you?" she pleaded.

"Why, certainly, darling," he answered, the picture of devotion. The young nurse smiled, and Sherri felt her temper start to rise.

"Bye, Miles," she called after him.

"Miles?" the nurse echoed uncertainly.

Sherri took pleasure in his warning look. "You wait for me, baby doll," she taunted further.

The nurse almost giggled, but restrained herself with an obvious effort. "Well, Miss Landers, you must be feeling better," was all she would say. "Now I'm going to page the doctor."

"Would you ask him if I can have something to eat?" Sherri asked. "I'm hungry."

The nurse beamed. "That's a very positive sign. And I'm sure the doctor will allow you a meal," she said as she bustled out of the room.

Sherri sank back onto the pillows. She couldn't wait for the doctor to be done with her so she could talk to Barrett again. But by the time the doctor and nurse were through examining her, Sherri was exhausted. She couldn't even stay awake for the promised dinner. In spite of her intentions, she fell into a deep, restful sleep.

The rain had stopped when she finally awoke, and it was completely dark outside. The light was on in her room; as before, Barrett sat in the chair by the window, gazing out.

Sherri squinted against the light. "What time is it?" she asked, attracting Barrett's attention.

"It's almost nine o'clock. How do you feel?"

"Overall, I feel better. My hands are bothering me, though." Sherri frowned. Her hands were throbbing, the result of a whole afternoon with no shots.

Barrett rang for the nurse; Sherri was beginning to wonder just how dependent on him she had become.

"Good evening, Miss Landers. I'm Katherine, your nurse for tonight. How can I help you?"

Sherri looked up into the friendly face of a woman who seemed familiar. "I know you," she said with conviction.

The woman, who was one of the older nurses, smiled. "And well you should," she said, taking a grandmotherly attitude toward Sherri. "I've been with you almost every night since you arrived. I was afraid you wouldn't remember me." She patted Sherri's arm. "Now, my dear, what can I do for you?"

"My hands hurt," she answered. "But I don't want those shots anymore. Do you think I could have something that doesn't knock me out quite so badly?"

"The doctor wrote some new medication orders for you. We were hoping you'd be ready for tablets soon." Katherine fussed over Sherri, smoothing her covers and plumping her pillows.

"I never had my dinner," Sherri recalled. "And I'm hungry!"

"You ought to be, my dear. All you've had to eat lately has come through this tube," the nurse said as she checked the IV bottle. "She could use filling out, right, Mr. Barrett?"

Barrett's eyes roamed over the bustline the thin hospital gown couldn't quite conceal. "She looks just fine to me."

Katherine chuckled wholeheartedly at Barrett's appreciative grin, and Sherri blushed. She would have pulled the covers up higher by grabbing the material between her two mittens, as she was beginning to think of her bandages, but her hands were hurting too much.

"Could I please have those pills?" she asked politely, but there was an urgency behind the request, which Katherine recognized, and the nurse hurried from the room.

"You seem to be quite popular with the nurses," Sherri observed, trying to ignore her hands.

"Actually, you're the one they're fond of. I'm just riding on the coattails of your popularity."

"Me?" Sherri was incredulous. "I can't believe that."

Barrett snorted. "Sherri, this isn't the ranger station. The nurses are really impressed with you. You've been a model patient, considering the circumstances."

"Really? I—"

"—don't remember," Barrett finished for her. "But you have. All that screaming aside, of course," he added wryly.

"Thanks," Sherri said, suspecting that she was being baited. "You must be right. They certainly wouldn't be falling all over your lovable personality."

Barrett laughed aloud, then covered his mouth, choking back the noise so as not to disturb other patients across the hall. "You must be feeling better," he commented. "Now I'm recognizing the Landers we all love to hate."

Their banter came to an end when Katherine returned with Sherri's pills and some dinner.

"What is this?" Sherri asked as she surveyed the tray before her.

"It's custard, gelatin, beef broth and tea," the nurse explained.

"What kind of dinner is that?" Sherri wailed.

"One that won't upset your stomach," Katherine informed her. "Gradually we'll get you back to hamburgers and fries, but in the meantime you'll have to settle for this. Now, do you want me to feed you, or do you want your boyfriend here to do the honors?"

"I'll take..." *You* was what Sherri started to say.

"Me, of course," Barrett broke in, and Sherri gave him a worried glance.

"Don't worry, darling, I may not be a nurse, but I can manage a spoon. We'll be fine, Katherine."

"All right. Take your pills, Sherri, then I'll be off. Just ring when you're done." Then she was gone.

"How about starting with the beef broth?" Barrett asked matter-of-factly, effectively subduing Sherri's worries that he would have fun at her expense.

"That's fine. But I feel so silly," she said as he offered her a spoonful of the clear liquid.

"You shouldn't. It beats having dinner out of an intravenous bottle." He moved closer to her with the next spoonful.

Sherri swallowed. "I suppose. I never stopped to realize how much we need our hands for." She took another swallow and grimaced. "This is awful."

"I'm sure it is. But if you finish everything up like a good girl, then I'll tell you all about our hospital romance." He winked, his mood suddenly lighthearted, and Sherri nearly choked.

Barrett lifted one eyebrow in amusement, as she suddenly couldn't finish eating fast enough. He gently wiped her lips, then set the dishes aside.

"Are those pills working yet?" he inquired.

"Lovely," Sherri admitted. Her hands barely hurt anymore, and although she was relaxed, she didn't feel sleepy or drugged.

"Good. Now, who wants to talk first? You or me?" Barrett's tone was light, but he seemed uneasy.

"Why don't you explain, and I'll listen?" Sherri suggested. "And face me, so I can see if you're lying."

Barrett chuckled at that. "Thanks for the confidence in my reputation as a gentleman." He laughed, not taking offense at all. "There. Satisfied?" he asked as he repositioned the chair. "I can turn on a brighter light, too, if you want. This can be an official interrogation."

"That won't be necessary," Sherri murmured, uncomfortable with the thin, too-revealing hospital gown. She would have to get some proper nightgowns and a robe, she decided, and soon.

"Fine." Suddenly Barrett's light mood was gone, and he was serious again. "Where to start?" he mused. Sherri didn't prompt him; after a long moment, he finally began.

"Yes, I told Holden we were engaged. I didn't have any choice. I felt awful about your injuries, especially after that stunt you pulled with the rope."

Sherri shifted uneasily, hoping Barrett would gloss over that in deference to her condition. But he didn't.

"Of all the stupid, foolhardy things to pull, and I've seen a lot of them in my day, yours takes the cake. I've seen plenty of brave actions in my life. I've also seen a lot of idiotic gestures made in the name of courage. I still haven't decided which category yours falls into, but, considering you've suffered enough and considering everything turned out pretty well in the end—excluding your hands—I'm prepared to let matters lie. Did you know you're going to get a medal for bravery?"

Barrett answered his own question. "No, you wouldn't re-member. Kevin and Rob's parents came to thank me and wanted to see you too, but you weren't in any condition at the time. Both boys are back home now. Holden gave me my commendation, for what it's worth, and you'll get yours later. Full ranger ceremony and all."

"Really?" Sherri's eyes were shining. "Do you have any pictures of yourself?"

"Don't be absurd." Barrett brushed off her request, but he was clearly touched that she was interested. "All I want out of that award is a little added push for my next promotion. But I'm getting off the subject."

"Yes, you are," Sherri agreed. "Did I forget about any-thing else besides my commendation—like our engagement?" she asked in pretended innocence.

Barrett's eyes narrowed slightly. "Don't get cute with me, Landers. When I carried you back to the horses, I was terribly worried about you. When I saw you lying there in the first-aid room, I remembered you had no relatives. I knew that if I was hurt, my whole family would flock to the hospital. I didn't feel it was right for you to be all alone, especially since your father had just died. Well, you know the rules. I couldn't come with you unless we were related, and being engaged was the best I could do on such short notice."

"I see," Sherri said stiffly, her face flushing with embar-rassment. He was worried about her, as he had put it, and he felt sorry for her. The only thing she couldn't stand more than people's dislike was their pity.

"And you didn't have to worry about finding a new part-ner. In addition to getting a nice vacation." Sherri didn't try to hide the bitter sarcasm in her voice. She averted her head, too upset to look Barrett in the eye.

"Sherri, don't," he urged. "We're both intelligent people, and I'm not going to lie to you. Yes, I felt...feel...compassion for you. And admiration. I've had a lot of partners and you're the best. And yes, I'd rather keep you as my partner than have anyone else. We work well together. But please don't try to read any more or any less into my motives. Be honest. Would you rather have been here in this hospital all alone, with no one to care about you, no friends to visit you? Granted, I'm no woman's prize, but I'm better than nothing.'' He spoke with conviction, and Sherri suddenly felt ashamed of herself.

"I appreciate your kindness,'' she said. And she meant it. "Like I told you, I don't remember much, but what I remember the most is your keeping me company. Thank you.''

Barrett said nothing, and after a while Sherri was able to lift her face to his. "But I'm much better. So what happens now? In other words, who dumps whom?'' she said bluntly. "I'll break it off first,'' she quickly offered. "No need for you to be thought of as the man who abandoned a sick woman.'' Somehow the thought of her co-workers intensifying their campaign against Barrett was a painful one.

"No.''

"You want to pretend to leave me? But Barrett, the other rangers will crucify you. Heaven knows they dislike you enough already,'' Sherri protested.

"No, not that either,'' Barrett said quietly, his green eyes fathoms deep with meaning.

"Then what...?'' Sherri was confused. "Barrett, I'm not up to guessing games.''

"It isn't hard to figure out, partner. There's a third solution. We stay engaged, and we follow through with marriage.''

"What?'' Sherri sat straight up in the bed, then regretted it as her head started to spin from the abrupt change of posture.

"Lean back, Landers,'' Barrett commanded, "or you're going to pass out. You haven't been up and about for three weeks. Take it easy!''

Sherri sank back against the pillows, and the dizziness subsided.

"It's been a long time since my charms have knocked a woman off her feet,'' Barrett observed, but the humor was forced. "Better? Good. Now before you start spouting off again, let me explain.'' He stood up and walked over to the window to close the curtains. For a moment, Sherri wondered if he was nervous about facing her, but that impression vanished as soon as he turned around.

Barrett leaned his large frame against the window sill, his health and vitality so obviously out of place in a sickroom. Sherri felt a flash of envy; right now, she couldn't even walk across the room unassisted, let alone perform any daring rescues.

"The way I see it," Barrett said, "is that we have one of two choices. We go our separate ways and suffer, or we make our team a permanent one. If we call off the engagement, I go back to a new partner in the mountains. You, on the other hand, will end up doing light duty in some gift shop at a park tourist attraction while you convalesce. Who knows how long that could be? Your hands will heal eventually, but you aren't going to pass any rope-climbing tests for quite a while. By the time you're certified fit for duty, I'll probably be stuck with some loser, and you'll get some awful partner of your own. Remember, no one wants to work with heroes and heroines, especially ones with medals. It's too hard on the ego." His movements easy and relaxed, Barrett came closer to sit on the edge of her bed.

"They could always team us up again," Sherri protested.

"Nonsense," Barrett snorted. "Besides, I'm up for promotion, and that means another rotation. I don't have enough seniority to choose where I go like you do, and we'll end up miles apart. Then we can kiss our partnership goodbye for good."

Sherri listened with a sinking feeling. He was right, so far. But marriage? She must have spoken aloud, because Barrett answered.

"Why not? You said you wanted to get married again, that you were tired of being alone. Where do you plan to find this future husband? At the ranger station?" The words were brutally clear: there, no man would go near her.

"At some gift shop among the tourists?" Barrett pressed on. "Or maybe you'll have a wild romance with another patient you meet in the hospital solarium," he suggested sarcastically. "Just like in the movies."

"All right, all right. My prospects aren't so good right now," Sherri admitted reluctantly.

"And how do you propose to go about changing them? You can't afford to quit and take an ocean cruise to stalk the perfect mate. Neither can I. We're stuck with our jobs if we want to make a living, and that's the truth. Why don't we accept the fact that there's a good rapport between the two of us and just settle for each other?" Barrett rose from the bed, as if he didn't want to see her eyes while she answered. "At least we're compatible," he threw in for good measure.

"But you don't love me! And I don't love you!" Sherri said the first, most obvious thing that popped into her head.

"So who needs love?" he said coldly. "I was in love once, and all it got me was a 'Dear John' letter. And look at yourself. Your husband left you a widow because his love for you couldn't compete with his love for excitement. Who needs it?" he repeated.

"Look at the advantages, Sherri. We'd be good company for each other. I'd be a considerate, faithful husband to you. And we'd have as many children as you desire." He paused. "It would be nice to share my bed with a woman again. It's been a long time," he said with a frankness that had Sherri lowering her eyes at his hunger. "Or would you rather become the station untouchable again? Because that's what will happen when you get out of here and eventually go back to work for Holden. Only we won't have each other around for moral support."

As abruptly as he'd broached the subject, he dropped it. "Just give the idea some thought." He spoke lightly, in a tone that could have been used to discuss the day's weather. "And now, I guess you'd better get some sleep. Good night, Landers," he said. Only this time he didn't touch her as he left.

BARRETT'S WORDS HAUNTED SHERRI as the days passed. She grew better and better and soon the doctors were speaking of discharging her and continuing her therapy as an outpatient. On several occasions, officials from the park service came around with papers to complete. Sherri knew that the time for a decision was drawing closer. There wasn't much to choose between, she thought ruefully. A loveless marriage, with companionship for herself and physical gratification for Barrett, or a lonely existence as the skilled and respected forest ranger, avoided by her co-workers.

The nurses found Sherri deeply troubled and unsettled more than once, and they tried to assure her that her scarred, stiff hands would eventually function again. But that wasn't it; what frightened Sherri was the thought of a loveless, solitary life. Some nights she dreamed it was she, and not her father, who had died alone in the mountains, with her body left to crumble in the wilderness. She would wake up shaking with fright.

Sherri knew she was a worthwhile person, a lovable person, but she realized she didn't know how to show that to others. The nurses seemed to like her, but that was when she'd been helpless and sick. Would they still like her as the aggressive, skilled ranger who didn't care about others' feelings or opinions when there was a life to be saved?

Barrett did, Sherri knew. He accepted her for what she was, and that might not be love but it was certainly better than nothing. A lot better.... Slowly her mind came to that conclusion on its own, for Barrett didn't press her; he simply continued in his role as devoted companion.

"The doctor tells me he's releasing you at the end of the week," Barrett said one day.

It was lunchtime, and Sherri was struggling to feed herself. The TV in the room was tuned to her favorite soap opera, and Barrett reached over to cut her meat for her as the heroine of the show was having a fight with her latest boyfriend.

"How can you watch this stuff?" Barrett asked her in disgust. "That woman will never get a husband if she keeps it up."

"That's where you're wrong," Sherri answered. "She's had five already: Jeff, Phil, Tom, Adam and Mike. So there." She gave up on the fork and switched to a spoon. Her fingers were just too clumsy to spear food onto the fork.

"I can't see how any intelligent person can watch this garbage." The end credits came up and Barrett switched off the set with relief.

"I haven't watched it for ages, and besides, even if I watched it every day, that doesn't mean I'm not intelligent. I enjoy the outrageous plots and the exaggerated characters."

"You must be pretty desperate for entertainment," Barrett said, but his remark was softened by the smile he threw her way.

Instead of lying weakly on the bed, Sherri was sitting comfortably in a chair with her lunch tray on a table. The skin on her face was smooth now, and the shiny, shoulder-length hair added a new touch of sophistication. The burns on her legs had healed with little scarring, and in a few more months, would barely be visible. Her figure under the lounging pajamas was thinner than it used to be, but her strength was returning, and except for her pitiful hands, Barrett was satisfied with what he saw.

"So what are your plans when you get discharged?" Barrett took the empty tray from her stiff fingers and placed it on the tray rack out in the hall.

Sherri paused, uncertain of how to express herself. "Maybe we should decide what *our* plans are," she said quietly. "Unless you've changed your mind, of course."

Barrett whirled around and looked at her sharply. "Does this mean what I think it means?"

"Yes," Sherri said simply. "If you still want me, I'll marry you."

Barrett smiled a slow smile that almost, but didn't quite, show in his eyes. "Well, well," he murmured. "It looks as if I have a fiancée after all." He quickly crossed the room to brush her cheek with an easy kiss. "I'm honored."

"Don't be ridiculous, Barrett," Sherri chastened, some of her old fire returning.

"But young men in love are supposed to act ridiculous," he answered smoothly.

"You're hardly young." *And you're not in love,* she added to herself.

"Ouch!" Barrett clutched his chest with one hand. "You've stabbed me to the quick."

"I'm beginning to regret this already," Sherri muttered, trying not to laugh at his melodramatic response.

"Now you're being ridiculous," Barrett said, businesslike once again. "What did you expect, springing your news on me in the middle of a hospital? Candlelight, flowers and a diamond ring?"

Sherri held up her crippled hands and looked at them sadly. "I don't think I'll be wearing much jewelry either way."

Barrett studied her for a long moment, his face intent. Finally he said, "We have a lot of planning to do. My new set of orders is coming up, then yours, and we have a wedding to arrange. Any preferences I should take into consideration?"

Sherri dropped her hands into her lap and smiled, unwilling to have Barrett think she was feeling sorry for herself. "For starters, you can tell Holden that I'm willing to be sent wherever you are, and that they can disregard my seniority for the time being. And since I have no family, of course I want to be married in your hometown. That's it."

"That's it?" Barrett asked. "Don't you want to see where I'm being sent first? You may not like it."

"It doesn't make any sense for us to be married if we aren't together," Sherri said practically. "If you could arrange to have my horses and the rest of my things sent on, that's all I want."

Barrett couldn't believe that she didn't have more preferences and desires. "What about the wedding? What kind of ceremony would you like?"

"It doesn't matter, although a church ceremony would be nice. Whatever you want is fine with me, and I'm sure that your mother and sister would be happy to offer suggestions. I've been married once before and you haven't, so I think it's only fair that you should have the final say. I'll even let you pick my dress."

"But that's bad luck!" Barrett insisted, and Sherri's eyes narrowed with speculation.

"You're acting like a nervous groom already. Frankly, I'm surprised you're such a traditional type." Under Sherri's sardonic gaze Barrett seemed to pull himself together.

"It's just that this wasn't what I expected," he said, clearing his throat. "I'd better get going, then. I have a lot of work to do. I'll see you later this evening, Landers."

Sherri rose to follow him out the door. "If we're going to be engaged, shouldn't you call me Sherri all the time now? I don't think *partner* or *Landers* is going to sit too well with your parents."

"Right." Barrett had by now regained most of his calm, assured manner. "And you'll have to call me—" he swallowed hard "—Miles. Damn, I hate that."

"Maybe I can think of something else for private. But I promise not to call you Miles in front of anyone except your family," Sherri offered kindly.

"Thanks." Barrett gave her a kiss on the lips that took her by surprise. He was certainly offering a good imitation of a loving future spouse. "Do you want a diamond or some other stone?" he asked casually.

"You really don't have to bother," Sherri insisted. "I won't be able to wear a ring for a long time. Besides, I wouldn't even know what size to buy, what with the scarring and all."

"Or did you intend to wear your old wedding ring?" Barrett's eyes were as cold as on that first day he had barged into her cabin, and Sherri shivered at the many moods this one man seemed to possess.

"No, Barrett. Thomas never bought me a ring. He said they were unnecessary symbols. I've never had a wedding band," Sherri informed him.

"No ring?" Barrett was incredulous. "The man must have been—" He paused and took a deep breath; Sherri saw the burning embers in his eyes flicker and die out as he regained control of himself.

"Don't you worry," Barrett told her mildly as he opened the door to her room. "You'll have your ring. I'll see you for dinner. Wear something pretty," he added as an afterthought. Then he was gone.

# CHAPTER SEVEN

SHERRI TOOK ANOTHER SIP of her coffee while she waited for Barrett to return from the airline's ticket counter. Their flight out of Denver's Stapleton airport had been delayed, and Barrett was checking to see how much longer they would have to wait. She looked down at her wrist and once again admired the bracelet that Barrett had given her during that memorable dinner in the hospital. The bracelet consisted of three gold strands, each woven through a gold ring, which sat on her wrist where a watch face might. In the center of the ring, anchored among the strands of gold that passed through it, was a solitaire diamond.

Sherri had been dazzled by the diamond's brilliance and size, and by the artistry of the bracelet. She knew that it must have been custom ordered—and that it must have cost a fortune. She was flattered by the extravagance of the gesture and she was deeply touched by it.

She remembered how the two of them had eaten dinner off hospital trays in the solarium. As he'd requested, Sherri had worn "something pretty." It wasn't a dress but a new caftan that she'd bought in the hospital gift shop and had intended to use as a robe. The shapeless, flowing garment didn't do much for her figure, but it had no buttons or zippers, and at least she could dress herself without assistance. Painstakingly she had combed her chocolate-colored hair, pleased to note that soft waves had appeared in the shorter layers, curls that had been straightened by the weight of her earlier waist-length style.

Barrett had told her about his meeting with an official from the forest service regarding their future orders.

"We should find out by the end of the week where we're headed, but I think I may have convinced them to send me to Oregon," he said, satisfaction in his voice.

"That's your home state," Sherri recalled with surprise. "How did you manage that?"

Barrett made a face at the lumpy gravy on his plate and decided to eat his meat without it. "The forest rangers are a national organization, and Oregon has a number of parks with positions I could fill," he said, as if explaining sums to a child.

"I know that," Sherri said impatiently. "I mean how did you manage an out-of-state transfer with only three years in service?"

"I explained we were getting married, and that we wanted the same duty station. I also explained that you had no family, and I wanted you near mine while you were convalescing. I told them if that couldn't be arranged, then they should be prepared to pay for round-the-clock care for you." Barrett smiled with smug satisfaction. "They grasped the economics of the situation right away."

Sherri sat quietly, trying to remember what little she knew of Oregon. It was amazing how these recent events in her life seemed almost predetermined, amazing how quickly they'd fallen into place. Barrett was certainly a fast worker when he had a mind to be.

"You look very nice this evening, Landers," Barrett said admiringly. He had fallen into the old name pattern.

"Thank you." Sherri was genuinely pleased. "I'm not up to using makeup yet, though." She was lucky if she could grasp a toothbrush long enough for the time it took to clean her teeth, but she didn't add that.

"Here. This is for when you want to dress up a bit." He casually handed her the jeweler's box containing the bracelet. Sherri couldn't open the box with its tight springs, and Barrett had to help her.

"I promised you a ring, didn't I?" he said as Sherri gasped.

"Is this for me?" Her eyes were wide with disbelief.

Barrett's eyes were kind as he released the bracelet from the clips that held it to the velvet backing. "Of course it is. Here, let me put it on for you. Since we're engaged, you can wear it on your right hand. Then when we're married, you can switch it to your left. We can always take the bracelet apart and have the diamond mounted on the ring later on, when your hands get better. I'll order a matching band to complete the set."

He slipped it carefully on her wrist. "There. It looks perfect on you."

To Sherri's embarrassment, tears formed in her eyes. He'd been so thoughtful; he needn't have done this.

"Why are you crying?" Barrett asked, still holding her scarred hand gently. "Is this the tough ranger that others live in fear of?"

His words put a stop to Sherri's tears. She couldn't admit that it had been years since she'd received any gifts. Instead, she chose to answer him in a like vein.

"Just the thought of tearing apart this lovely bracelet brought tears to my eyes," Sherri said in a shaky voice. "Thank you."

Barrett watched her sharply. "For a minute there, I thought you were going to give it back and say that it wasn't the real you. I know I don't have much practice in picking out gifts for women," he said uneasily.

"No. No, Miles, it's beautiful. I love it." Sherri continued to admire the bracelet on her wrist, glad of the heavy safety chain that would let her wear it without worry.

"Good." Barrett was his usual brisk self again, and the evening had ended soon after.

So had her stay at the hospital. In less time than she would have thought possible, she had received her discharge papers, her new orders and sick-leave papers, appointments for therapy and follow-up at an Oregon hospital and airline tickets for Portland. Barrett personally packed her bags and arranged for Janet to send the rest of her clothes, still at the ranger station, to his parents' home. The horses would arrive a month later.

If anyone had told her three months ago that she'd be on a plane to Portland with her future husband, she would have burst out laughing. Now it was actually happening—and she could hardly believe it herself. Looking up, she saw Barrett approaching, head above the crowd, and she let the cuff of her sleeve fall back over the bracelet.

"What a mess," Barrett said with disgust. "Sorry I took so long."

"That's all right." Sherri pushed away the Styrofoam coffee cup. "What's the latest news?"

Barrett settled down into the chair beside her in the airport lobby. "All they'll say is that they're having mechanical trouble. It appears that whatever the problem is, it can't be fixed. We're going to have to wait until they unload our original plane, and reload all the luggage onto an alternate. With luck, we'll be getting out of here soon after that.

"Airlines," Barrett snorted. "Just once I'd like to book a flight for a certain time and actually have it leave then." He stopped his tirade and studied Sherri's face for signs of discomfort. "So, how are you holding out?"

"Fine. I'm kind of disappointed, though. I was looking forward to my first flight. I should have bought a paperback at the gift shop to help pass the time." She'd originally intended to do that, but had decided against it, assuming they'd be leaving shortly.

"You've never flown before?" Barrett was obviously astounded.

"No. Well, I take that back. I did fly in the helicopter to the hospital, but I was asleep all the way, so I'm not counting that. I wish we were being delayed on account of the weather instead of engine problems, though." Sherri shifted uneasily in her chair. She did have a slight case of preflight jitters, although she wouldn't admit it.

"I never would have guessed," Barrett muttered, shaking his head. "We've been sitting in the lobby all this time, and you haven't complained once. I just assumed you were a seasoned traveler."

"I've never been out of the state of Colorado. And as for sitting quietly, I did a lot of that when Dad left me alone at the cabin to go prospecting. I got used to it." Sherri was watching the crowds of people go by, and she missed the penetrating look that Barrett gave her.

He started to say something, then changed his mind and just said, "I hope we don't miss our connection in Los Angeles. I couldn't get us a nonstop flight; they were all sold out because of some big convention in Portland." He didn't tell Sherri, but he was worried that the day might prove too long for her. She still tired easily, and even the healthiest person could emerge limp and weary after long hours of traveling.

"Do you want to find a hotel and start again tomorrow, Landers? I mean Sherri," he corrected himself. "We've been here for three hours already, and who knows how much longer we're going to have to wait. Then there's still the connecting flight ahead."

"I'm fine," Sherri insisted. "Maybe I'll get that book after all, though, for the plane."

"Well, if you're sure . . ."

"Really," Sherri insisted. He certainly seemed concerned about her, but sitting in a chair wasn't wearing her out, and she had her tablets in case her hands started to hurt.

"Would you like me to go and buy a book for you?" he suggested. "The crowds are pretty heavy, and someone might accidentally bump into your hands."

"I could stay with the bags," she said slowly, for she and Barrett only had carry-on luggage. "But you don't know what I want!"

Barrett rose easily to his feet, towering over her and the other waiting passengers. "After seeing the kind of television you watch," he said, referring to her soap opera, "I can imagine what you read. Let me guess—mushy books with pictures of swashbuckling heroes tearing the bodices off lovely young maidens on the cover." He leered in an excellent imitation of some of the more lurid paperback covers, and Sherri suppressed a chuckle.

"Don't be ridiculous," she said with dignity. "Although there's nothing wrong with those books if they entertain you."

"Ah-ha, so you do read them," Barrett pounced.

"Sometimes," Sherri admitted stiffly, color coming to her cheeks. "But I'm really in the mood for a good mystery. And please, Barrett, not too much blood and gore in it. Something along the lines of Agatha Christie would be nice."

"I'll do my best, but this is the airport, not a proper bookstore, and they don't cater to the prudent reader, you know," he warned.

"Just do your best." She watched his tall form blend into the crowd and smiled. But her smile faded as the doubts she'd been able to bury under the excitement of the trip began to surface. Again Sherri had to wonder about the wisdom of her decision.

Had she really been so desperate for acceptance that she could consider settling for a loveless marriage with a virtual stranger? Had Thomas's death and then her father's left her so defenseless against the world that an offer from another social misfit would be welcome? Well, the answer was obvious. She was wearing Barrett's ring on her wrist, its unconventional location a sign of their unconventional match. Still, children were something to look forward to. Sherri blushed at the thought. She had never engaged in casual sex; she'd never been with anyone but Thomas. She had to admit that there had been real sparks between her and Barrett, though. So maybe—

The sound of the lobby's loudspeaker interrupted her reverie.

"Attention, please. All passengers bound for flight 137 to Los Angeles . . . boarding will begin at gate thirteen in ten minutes."

Sherri hoped that Barrett had heard the announcement. She wouldn't board unless he did, and after all the time they'd spent waiting, it would be a shame if they didn't make the flight. She needn't have worried though; Barrett rejoined her a few moments later, plastic bag in hand.

"I heard," he said as she explained that they should be getting ready to board. "Here's your book. It may not be to your taste, but it was the best I could do with what they had."

Sherri smiled her thanks, and soon they were finally boarding. To Sherri, the actual takeoff was something of a disappointment. In fact, compared to some of the rescues she'd handled, it felt downright dull. True, it was a novelty to see everything recede, becoming tinier and tinier below them, but she could accomplish the same thing by climbing any of her favorite mountain trails.

"You don't seem nervous," Barrett observed, and Sherri explained why.

Then, in a wistful voice, she added, "The only thing that affects me is leaving home. I've never been away before. I wonder when I'll see it again." Sherri thought of her parents' graves, alone and untended up in the mountains.

Barrett reached for her forearm and gently squeezed it. "You have a home with me now. We'll go back as often as we can manage it."

Sherri nodded, feeling a little better. But she still shivered as the plane rose above the cloud cover and the Colorado Rockies disappeared from her sight.

THE FLIGHT WAS LONG, tedious and draining. The food was cold, the flight bumpy due to turbulence, and the overall attitude of the passengers was one of weariness. Even the flight attendants gave up trying to paste false smiles on their own faces. When the captain announced that all flights out to San Diego, Portland and Seattle had been canceled as a result of heavy fog in Los Angeles, half the plane groaned aloud.

Barrett himself cursed, and Sherri sighed with frustration. "Well, at least we don't have to worry about missing our connecting flight," she said, trying to lighten their moods.

"The end result is the same," Barrett said irritably. "I have no intention of sitting in the terminal all night waiting for the fog to lift. And I can just imagine what it's going to be like finding a hotel." Barrett rang for the stewardess to take away his coffee.

"I was hoping for a good dinner at my parents' house and a comfortable bed. We'll be lucky to find either of those in L.A." Barrett rubbed his forehead. He was exhausted and stiff in every limb; he could imagine how Sherri felt.

"How are you doing?" he asked.

Sherri gave him a weak smile, uncertain of whether to tell him the truth, and Barrett noticed her hesitation.

"Come on, let's hear it." His green eyes were stern; Sherri leaned close to him to whisper in his ear.

"I have a problem," she admitted, her face a flushed red. "I need to go to the ladies' room, but..." Here she gestured helplessly toward herself.

"But what?" Barrett wondered.

"The nurses dressed me this morning. I can't unbuckle my belt, or unbutton the top of my jeans. I might be able to manage the zipper. Barrett, don't look like that! I knew I shouldn't have said anything!" Sherri turned her burning face away from him. She couldn't bear to see the amused grin tugging at the corners of his mouth.

"It isn't funny," she hissed.

"No wonder you've been squirming in your seat the past half hour." Barrett chuckled at her indignant look. "No problem, I'll just come with you, undo your pants, and wait by the door until you're done."

"Forget it!"

"Then ask one of the stewardesses to help you," Barrett suggested.

Sherri shook her head. They'd want to know why, then they'd see her hands and ask the inevitable questions. "I don't want to have to give them my life story," she said softly after glancing around to make sure no one was eavesdropping on their conversation.

"It's either one of them or me. Come on, Landers, think of it as a warm-up for our wedding night." He flinched in mock terror as Sherri hit him hard with her paperback.

"That's not amusing," she said, loudly enough for several heads to turn her way. She sat there stonily, considering her alternatives. "I just won't go," she finally announced.

Barrett shrugged, but she could tell he was silently fighting his laughter. "Suit yourself, but it's been a long day, and it's going to be an even longer evening. Mind if I borrow that book?"

Sherri threw him the paperback, a murder mystery with terribly mangled bodies and an investigator who seemed to be in the book for the sole purpose of bedding as many of the female suspects as the author could manage. She tried to think of things other than her pressing discomfort, but it wasn't easy. She felt so helpless! Until she regained movement in her fingers, she would have to suffer the loss of her dignity in order to accomplish even such simple, basic tasks as going to the ladies' room. A tear spilled down her right cheek, and then her left. And she had promised herself that she wasn't going to cry. Barrett would really taunt her now.

She furtively wiped away the tears, hoping Barrett would be too engrossed in the book to notice. He wasn't. He slipped the book into the pocket of the seat in front of him, then stood up. Clasping her arm, he pulled her up, and with an inclining motion of his head, signaled for her to follow him. They went carefully down the narrow aisle to the back restroom. Barrett opened the door for her, and using it to block the other passengers' view, silently unbuckled her belt and unbuttoned her jeans.

"Take your time," he said softly. "Just knock lightly when you're ready, and I'll fasten you up." He took in Sherri's miserable expression. "It'll be easier for you to ask the next time, if that's any consolation."

As the tears continued to fall, Barrett reached up and lightly stroked her hair. "I promise to buy you as many jeans with elastic waistbands as you can stuff in your suitcase, okay?" He gave Sherri a little push, then closed the door for her.

A man behind Barrett rudely asked, "Hey, what's the holdup, lady? Let's get going."

Sherri froze, her embarrassment even worse than before. On the other side of the door she heard Barrett say, "Unless you're planning on buying dentures in the next five seconds, buddy, I suggest you watch your mouth." There were slight sounds of a scuffle, then silence.

"Barrett?" she called.

The sound of his voice came through the door. "I'll be back in five minutes."

Sherri leaned her head against the door, one hand still holding up her jeans. She suddenly felt sick. This wasn't how she'd imagined her first flight. With a sudden resolve to do her therapy exercises faithfully, Sherri took care of her immediate need. The sooner she could dress herself, the better.

Barrett was back as quickly as he'd promised, and Sherri flinched at the sight of his tight face and blazing eyes as he fastened her up, then led her back to their seats. She knew his anger wasn't directed at her, and wondered what had become of the other man.

She was too embarrassed to ask or to attempt any kind of conversation, and besides, Barrett looked too formidable. His size was intimidating enough when he was cheerful; in a display of temper he was positively overpowering. He reminded her of the old pictures of frontiersmen, rugged, muscled, and absolutely fearless. What would he look like with a heavy beard? Probably unapproachable, she'd decided—the way he looked right now.

They sat in silence for the rest of the flight. Sherri managed to nap a little; when she woke up they were landing. It was late evening, and the damp, thick fog was everywhere. Since they didn't have to wait for luggage, Barrett was able to obtain a rental car immediately.

"There must be hotels around somewhere that have vacancies. We'll find one even if we have to try them all."

An hour later Sherri could have sworn that they had. They'd finally found an out-of-the-way motel that had a vacant room.

"All we have left is room 108, which only has one bed," the clerk said in response to Barrett's request for two rooms, or at least two beds.

Barrett sighed in frustration, and glanced over at Sherri for her reaction. "It's all they have, Sherri."

"You'd better take it," the clerk said. "The fog has closed down most of the flights out of here. Everything this side of town is filled up with airline passengers."

Sherri looked at Barrett's shadowed eyes and weary, drooping shoulders. "We'll take it."

Minutes later they were in their room. It was small and plain, but clean.

"Why don't you lie down on the bed and stretch out for a bit while I clean up?" Sherri suggested.

Barrett tossed the suitcases on the floor. "That sounds good to me. Do you need any help with the faucets?"

"No, those I can manage. But these..." She gestured toward her jeans. "If you would do the honors..." she said, standing in front of him.

Barrett did, then flopped back on the bed. "I'll call the airport in a few minutes and find out about our flight to Portland, then I'll call my parents. Holler if you need me." He threw one arm across his eyes and groaned. "Those seats were made for people five feet tall," he complained, "not for people like me." Within seconds, he was asleep.

Sherri watched him protectively, unfamiliar feelings stirring inside her. He had been taking care of her all day, but who ever took care of him? Gathering some clean clothes from her suitcase, she got into the shower, staying under the warm, driving water until she felt refreshingly clean. Then she pulled on her caftan, the one she'd worn the evening he gave her the bracelet.

Barrett was still asleep when Sherri left the bathroom. She awkwardly removed his shoes and socks, her actions not disturbing him at all. The phone in their room had push-buttons, so she was able to call and check on their flight to Portland. It wasn't due to leave until three in the morning, and that was only if the fog lifted. Sherri canceled it and made new reservations for nine the next morning. Then she clumsily flipped through the phone book's yellow pages until she found a pizza parlor that delivered. She was hungry, and she thought Barrett probably was, too. She hoped he liked pepperoni and mushrooms, because along with salads and soda, that was what she ordered.

Sherri debated waking Barrett up. She knew his parents would be waiting to hear from him, but he looked so peaceful that she was unwilling to disturb him. Drawn by a sudden impulse, she lay down on the bed beside him.

A knock on the door woke them both up. Sherri found herself in Barrett's arms, heart pounding at the sudden noise.

"Who in the world is that?" Barrett sat straight up, apparently accepting her presence in the bed with no more interest than if they'd been just two rangers sharing a tent while on assignment. Sherri was surprised to find herself feeling slightly insulted.

"It's our dinner," she answered as she struggled to a sitting position and pushed the hair out of her face. "Where's my purse?"

"I'll get it," Barrett said, his voice thick with sleep. He reached for his wallet and stumbled toward the door.

"One large mushroom and pepperoni pizza, two salads, Italian dressing, and two sodas?" the delivery boy asked.

Barrett looked toward Sherri, and she nodded. He paid, then set their dinner on the bed and opened the box for an appreciative sniff. "Mmm, this smells great."

"I should call the airport first," he said reluctantly as Sherri started her salad.

"I already did," she said between bites. "I canceled our delayed flight and rescheduled. We leave at nine tomorrow morning. So, unless you want to change that, dig right in."

Barrett flashed her a look of gratitude. "For this," he mumbled, his mouth full of pizza, "you have my undying devotion."

"You paid," she pointed out.

"That's right, I did. I should be thanking myself instead."
He grinned boyishly, and for a moment Sherri was taken aback
by his lightheartedness.

They sat cross-legged on the bed and ate contentedly, arguing indifferently over the last piece, which was rightfully Sherri's, as she was the slower eater. They decided to split it.

"I can't eat another bite," Sherri groaned as she swallowed
the last mouthful.

"Good thing you're wearing that loose caftan, then," Barrett teased, and Sherri tossed her wadded-up napkin at him.

"Shouldn't you call your parents?" she reminded him.

"Right. By the way," he drawled. "I haven't told my family
I'm getting married. Shall I do that now or surprise them when
we get there?" He watched her closely, trying to gauge her reaction.

"I don't want to suddenly appear on their doorstep and
expect them to put me up for the night, Barrett! For heaven's
sake, tell them! Unless you're having second thoughts," Sherri
added. She couldn't understand him. One minute he was so
likable, and the next he seemed to be deliberately trying to
provoke her.

"Second thoughts? Not me," he said, his voice slow and
husky. "Do you want proof?" He circled her waist, and in one
fluid motion pulled her close.

Barrett laughed softly as Sherri held herself stiffly away from
him. "I wouldn't struggle with those hands, my dearest wife-to-
be. They're only healed enough for soft caresses."

Covering her mouth with his, he let his weight force her back
onto the pillows. "You taste of pepperoni," he murmured.

Sherri angrily turned her head to one side, effectively breaking the kiss.

"What do you think you're doing?" she demanded.

"My dear partner, I'll give you three guesses." His eyes were
mocking, and although he didn't press his advantage, neither
was he about to let Sherri go.

"Just because we're sharing the same bed doesn't mean we're
going to do anything besides sleep." Sherri tried to push him

away, but her hands protested at the effort. Barrett kept her pinned beneath him, playing all the while with strands of her soft, glossy hair.

"Has it ever occurred to you," he asked in a low, teasing voice, "that maybe I'm tired of having you throw yourself at me? Oh, yes, you have," he insisted as Sherri started to deny his words.

"We always seem to end up in the same bed. First we shared the same sleeping bag, then later when mine dried out you still welcomed me in your tent."

"That was because you were stupid enough to lose your tent when it washed downstream! Next time you can sleep outside in the cold," Sherri vowed, infuriated by his taunting.

"And now here we are again," he continued, as though she hadn't spoken. "You practically jumped at the chance to get me alone in this bed. You could have refused. You know we could have kept on searching for another hotel." He nuzzled at her ear, and in spite of herself Sherri shivered with desire.

"You'd been driving forever, and I made the mistake of feeling sorry for you! Would you please get off me, you clumsy ox? You weigh a ton and I can't breath," Sherri complained, fearful that he might notice the sudden weakening of her resistance. Her body seemed to be slowly but relentlessly melting, reaching a boiling point of its own.

Barrett obligingly shifted his weight, and Sherri paled with pleasure as she felt his body moving against hers. Barrett laughed softly.

"And then there was that kiss. You remember...that sweet, ravishing kiss you gave me in front of the fire."

Sherri turned away from him, her face flushing at the memory.

"Now don't tell me you've forgotten," he chided softly, his green eyes glittering. "Remember how your hands were on my body, skin against skin? And how I had to push you away just to keep you under control?"

Sherri closed her eyes, and Barrett laughed again in triumph. "So you do remember," he said. He traced the outline of her hardened breasts under the caftan, the material rustling seductively.

"We *are* engaged," he urged as he unbuttoned his shirt with one hand and continued his explorations with the other.

"Yes, but . . ." Sherri gasped.

"And we aren't inexperienced, either, are we?" Barrett sat up and unbuckled his belt, still continuing his caresses between motions.

"No, but . . ."

"And you *have* been throwing yourself at me," Barrett went on. His pants were now falling to the floor, and Sherri moistened her lips as she realized that all he had on now was a tight pair of men's low-cut briefs that left nothing to the imagination.

"Have not," Sherri whispered. "Barrett, please get dressed."

"I promise to respect you in the morning." He laughed with a husky sound as the last piece of clothing fell to the floor. Sherri gasped at the sudden beauty of him.

Barrett carefully covered her with his body again, in no hurry to force her to a decision.

"You know, Landers, you've been married before, so I know you're not worried about honestly wearing white at our wedding. Could it be that you're the frigid old maid the station claims you are after all?"

He shifted slightly, and gently reached under her caftan. Ever so slowly, with teasing, downward motions, he pulled off her panties. By the time he had reached her knees she was breathing heavily. By the time the panties were freed from her ankles and tossed to the floor her upper lip was beaded with moisture.

"No, definitely not frigid," he said with a smile. His hand reached back under the caftan to stroke the inner surface of one thigh, and his own breath quickened as she trembled under his touch.

"I only agreed to this room because you looked so tired." She tried one last argument. "It had nothing to do with anticipating our wedding night."

"Practice makes perfect," Barrett insisted in her ear. He gently nipped at the lobe, then reached for the bottom hem of her caftan.

"Are you going to take this off, or shall I?"

Sherri tried to resist, but small things kept popping into her mind. Barrett eating meals with her, Barrett planting flowers on her father's grave, Barrett's smiles and jokes in the hospital. He made her feel so at peace with herself. He chased away her loneliness. And suddenly she realized that, most precious of all, he had given her the chance to love again. She loved him; she was suddenly so sure of it, and that love superseded such traditional decrees as waiting until after the wedding. She wanted to please him, and with a sudden surge of flame, she realized that she wanted him to please her.

"I'm waiting for an answer, Landers," Barrett pressed.

Slowly, hesitantly at first, and then with growing determination Sherri wound her arms around Barrett's neck and pulled him closer. Her face glowed softly with a radiance of its own as she memorized the features of the man above her.

"Sherri?" Barrett said uncertainly, a question in his eyes.

Sherri's lips curved upward in an ageless Mona Lisa smile, and she tilted back her head, inviting his kiss. She readily opened her lips, tasting the sweetness of his breath, inhaling the scent that was uniquely Barrett's.

For the first time in their relationship she had no desire to resist him or to fight with him, and Barrett instantly grasped the change in her reactions. He deepened his kiss, possessing her mouth with a leashed passion that strained to break free.

Sherri urged him on with her loving responses, desperate to feel him lose the arrogant self-control that was so much a part of him. She wanted all of him, or nothing at all, and as her caftan slipped to the floor and he hoarsely cried, "Oh, Sherri," she knew there would be no turning back for either of them.

LATER, WHEN THEY HAD RELUCTANTLY come back to the real world of hotel sheets and dim lights, Sherri turned to Barrett.

"I can't believe this." Her eyes were soft with wonder as she searched for the words to tell him how precious their union had been. But before she could gather her thoughts, Barrett interrupted.

"I told you we'd enjoy the physical side of marriage," he announced smugly. It almost sounded as if he was bragging, and Sherri flinched at the turn the conversation had taken.

"I certainly enjoyed myself," he was saying. "My compliments on your technique, Landers. Although as I mentioned before, it's been a long time between women for me."

Sherri's heart sank and a sick feeling flooded her stomach. So now she was Landers again, not Sherri. And their physical union hadn't been an expression of love on his part, the way it had been on hers. He just wanted physical satisfaction, pure and simple.

"Something wrong, Landers?" Barrett was watching her closely.

"No, no, nothing," she lied, masking her sorrow. "I'm glad you enjoyed yourself." She forced a yawn. "But I'm really very tired now. If you don't mind, I think I'll go to sleep." At least if the lights were off, he wouldn't see her desolation.

"It is late," Barrett agreed. "I think I'll go clean up. A hot shower would sure feel good." He swung out of bed and walked to the bathroom nude, as if she weren't even in the room.

Sherri swallowed hard, trying to get rid of the tight feeling in her throat. She waited until the bathroom door was closed before she put the caftan back on and burrowed under the covers. Sleep was a long time in coming, and by the time Sherri finally drifted off, Barrett still hadn't returned to bed. So she didn't see him standing there later, staring down at her for long minutes before he climbed in beside her and clicked off the light.

# CHAPTER EIGHT

THE FOG WAS NOWHERE to be seen the next morning, and Sherri and Barrett had no problem with their flight to Portland. Both were subdued on the plane, speaking politely to each other when necessary, and lost in their own thoughts the rest of the time. After a while Barrett roused himself, however, to acquaint Sherri with his family background.

Barrett's parents were Emily and Frank, Portland natives. They headed the family shipping business, which catered to the Oregon lumber industry. Originally Frank Barrett had operated his boats for local fishermen, but he soon found that transporting materials between the logging camps was far more lucrative. His business grew, and he was able to hire on two of his three children as assistants. Barrett, of course, had struck out on his own.

"After me, the next oldest is Roger," Barrett told her. "He has a wife and two boys. Roger is in charge of the fleet. My sister Felicity does the secretarial work, Mom does the bookkeeping, and Dad is the administrative brains behind it all."

"The name Roger doesn't sound as unusual as Miles and Felicity," Sherri observed, the first nonessential words she'd spoken to Barrett that morning.

"It's a proper Pilgrim name, all right. My sister and I weren't as lucky as my brother." Barrett grimaced. "My father hated it when my sister announced that she wanted to go by 'See.' It was the closest to a nickname she could come up with. I'm the only family member who calls her that, although that's how she's known to her school friends."

Sherri could sense the pride and love he felt for his sister. "What does she call you?" she wondered, hoping Barrett's sister could provide her with a more personal name for her partner. "She must know that you dislike your name, too."

Barrett smiled, his eyes growing soft. "She calls me Miles. My father's a strict parent, and See doesn't get away with much. He does a good job of hiding the fact that she's the apple of his eye. She's my parents' only daughter."

"It sounds as though you feel the same way about her," Sherri guessed.

Barrett readily admitted it. "My sister has always been special to me. Even as a child she went out of her way to make me happy. But I'm afraid she carries the big brother crush just a bit too far sometimes."

"And you love every minute of it. I'm sure she'll be overjoyed to have you home again." Sherri's sincere words seemed to ease some of the tension between them.

"It will be good to see her," Barrett replied affectionately. He became silent, his forehead furrowing in a troubled frown.

"What is it?" Sherri asked. No answer was forthcoming, and she shifted uncomfortably in her seat. Both of them had carefully avoided making any reference to last night, and for a moment Sherri was afraid she had opened that forbidden topic.

"I didn't mean to pry," she said in an effort to make amends, but Barrett hadn't been offended.

"You aren't. I was just trying to remember when I was home last." He shook his head. "It seems like forever."

Sherri blinked in surprise. "Couldn't you get the time off?" She knew that ranger stations in remote areas had a generous vacation policy.

Barrett's lips twisted bitterly. "I could have, but I didn't." His voice warned against any further inquiries, but Sherri was too shocked to take heed.

"You didn't bother to go home at all?" she said incredulously. "But Barrett, why ever not? Don't you get along with your family?" Her face was full of concern.

"We get along fine," was the curt answer. He threw her an accusing glance. "Trust you to twist the knife a little deeper, my dear."

Sherri hated to see him returning to the hostile defensiveness that had been suppressed during her recuperation, but she refused to back down.

"I wasn't accusing you," she said reproachfully. "I'm just trying to understand your behavior. It doesn't make any sense."

"I have no intention of discussing my family's affairs with you in front of a planeload of other people. Besides, none of this is any of your business."

Sherri drew an angry breath. "Excuse me, but may I remind you that I'm going to be a member of your family? Although I'm beginning to doubt the wisdom of that decision," she said heatedly.

The conversation ended there, and the tension that had seemed to abate was now back in full force. The rest of the flight passed in silence, as did the first half of the taxi ride to Barrett's Portland home.

"Landers . . . Sherri," he finally said, "I'm sorry about earlier. I shouldn't have snapped at you."

"Don't worry about it." Sherri's calm voice hid the confusion she felt. "You were right. It really wasn't any of my business." She kept her head averted, pretending interest in the scenery outside her window.

Barrett's hand descended gently on her shoulder. "I suppose I should explain."

"That's not necessary. You made it quite clear that I was out of line." In spite of herself Sherri's skin warmed to his touch.

"I want to explain," Barrett persisted. He took a deep breath, as if to brace himself. "It's really very simple. Karen was from Portland, and the man she married was from Portland. I was always bumping into them, running into people that we'd all known, going places she and I had been together . . . It was just too much. I decided to leave Portland and all those memories behind. Even visiting my family brought out the worst in me. I wasn't doing anyone a favor with my presence, and I figured it was best for all concerned if I just stayed away."

His hand fell from her shoulder as Sherri turned to face him.

"That is the craziest logic I've ever heard!" Sherri burst out, and the driver glanced in his mirror to see what he was missing. A black stare from Barrett soon had him focusing his attention on the road again.

"Airplanes and taxis are not the greatest places for conversation," Barrett complained as he ran his fingers through his hair, leaving it in rumpled waves. Sherri smiled at the sight, and Barrett gave her a rueful answering grin.

Suddenly she felt free to speak her mind. "Barrett, did you ever think that maybe your family could have helped you? What's so terribly wrong with accepting a little comfort from them?"

Barrett didn't answer, and Sherri pressed on. "All you ended up doing was cheating your family and cheating yourself. You shouldn't take their presence for granted. Some day you may turn around and they won't be there for you. I'm glad you're going to see them again, even if the reasons for this visit were based on my situation and not yours."

Sherri stopped with dismay as a new thought surfaced. Stealing a glance at Barrett, she saw that he didn't seem angry or offended by her frankness. She decided to take a chance.

"What happens if you run into your old girlfriend again, Barrett? There's always that possibility, you know."

"I hadn't thought about it," Barrett said slowly.

"Come on now, surely you don't expect me to believe that?" Sherri scoffed.

"No, honestly," he assured her. "I've only thought about this trip home in terms of what was best for you. The thought of Karen never entered my mind," he said with growing realization and some surprise.

Some demon within her forced Sherri to continue. "And what if you run into her? What if she calls you up and wants to see you for 'old times' sake'?"

"I wouldn't be bothered one way or the other," Barrett insisted. "If I see her, fine; if not, that's fine, too."

Sherri was still not convinced. "If that's true, why haven't you bothered going home before now?" Her heart seemed to pause in the suspense of waiting for his answer. She prepared herself for anything but could not possibly have predicted his slow, honest words.

"Maybe I just never realized how unimportant Karen is until now."

Sherri's jaw dropped in surprise. "You are without a doubt the most contradictory man I have ever met," she finally said. Still, her eyes shone with pleasure over his answer.

"Perhaps," was all he would agree to, and for the moment, that was enough.

SHERRI SETTLED EASILY into the Barrett household. She didn't see much of Barrett's father or brother, since they were involved in running the family business and were frequently away. But Barrett's mother and sister made a special effort to spend time with Sherri and to make her feel at home. Soon after their arrival, Barrett had reported to the Portland office of the forestry service, arranging for an extended vacation to cover wedding preparations and a honeymoon. His new orders and duty station were not yet final.

Sherri thought that the uncertainty concerning his next job would be an annoying thorn in Barrett's side, but to her surprise he seemed unconcerned. For a man who always liked to be in control of things, Barrett's nonchalance was quite out of character. Barrett's family thought so, too, and they quickly attributed Barrett's new-found patience to Sherri's influence. Sherri was just as certain that it had nothing to do with her, but she wisely kept quiet; Barrett seemed truly happy for the first time since she'd met him.

His happiness at the reconciliation with his family spilled over onto her, and although she knew she wasn't the reason for his contentment, she was satisfied. Barrett did seem especially considerate and thoughtful of her wishes, and his family didn't doubt that they were an engaged couple deeply in love. Only Sherri knew the truth, but she consoled herself with the fact that Karen was never mentioned again. She could account for every minute of Barrett's time, for he was always either with her or with a member of his family. Gradually she came to accept Barrett's indifference to Karen, and while it wasn't the declaration of love she hoped and prayed for, at least it meant one less obstacle in her path.

Still, Sherri couldn't dispel the sense of unease that reared its head to torment her at the most unexpected times—times such as the relaxed, pleasant evenings she spent with the Barrett family. Everyone would gather after dinner to sit in the large parlor. Sherri would sit next to Barrett, his arm draped around her shoulders with the casual familiarity of a lover's. She would listen quietly to the conversation and imagine what it would be like to start her own family and have evenings like these in her own home.

It was on one of these evenings that the subject of what they would do after the wedding arose.

"Now Miles," Barrett's mother, Emily, chided, "I know we have the wedding all planned, but you haven't said a word about where you and Sherri are going to live afterward. It would certainly help us in preparing a gift list for you two."

"Mom's right," Felicity agreed. "Sherri, do you have your own furniture? And your own dishes and linens?"

"Are you going to buy a house or find an apartment?" Frank asked.

"I have no idea," Barrett answered. "It all depends on what area I'm assigned to with the rangers." His voice was sociable enough, but Sherri felt the tightening of his arm behind her neck.

"Haven't you heard anything yet?" Emily persisted. "It certainly complicates matters."

Barrett shrugged. "As long as we're married, that's all that matters for now."

Sherri looked up at him sharply, disturbed by his evasiveness. She didn't like the tight set of his jaw. "Miles, where *are* we going to live? I certainly don't want to set up housekeeping in a ranger cabin," she stated. "I'd like to find a place close to where we'd be working."

Barrett was obviously annoyed by her comments. "We're not even married yet and all you can think about is working. You haven't even recovered from your last mishap on the job," he said tersely, withdrawing his arm from her shoulders.

Sherri blinked in surprise at his vehemence. "But . . . I just want to make sure that our marriage plans and our careers mesh smoothly," she explained.

"If you were like any other woman you'd be fussing over wedding invitations and your trousseau instead of your career. If I had my way, you'd find some other line of work. Something safer." He looked pointedly at Sherri's hands.

The rest of the family went silent with embarrassment but Sherri was barely aware of them. "Miles, you know I intend to go back to work. Did you check about getting assigned to an area where I can easily join you later?" She was worried that he might be assigned to a location where position openings were few and far between, the way they were at her old ranger station.

"I wish you'd stop nagging me about that, Sherri," Barrett answered curtly.

"Son, there's no need for that kind of rudeness," Frank said in a quietly authoritative voice.

"The groom must be getting a case of prewedding nerves," Felicity joked, trying to relieve the tension in the room.

Barrett readily agreed, but Sherri noticed how forced his smile was, and how quickly he changed the subject.

Later on, when they were alone, she tried to talk to him again. "Barrett, what's the matter?" she asked. "And don't try to tell me you have a case of prewedding nerves, either. I'll never believe that one in a million years."

Barrett didn't answer her at first. He stood at the window, watching the last of the autumn leaves fly in the wind. The trees were nearly bare, and with sadness Sherri realized that fall was almost over. Back home in the mountains there would already be snow and a feeling of intense homesickness washed over her.

"Barrett?" she tried again.

This time he turned around and gave her his attention. "Maybe you're the one getting a case of the jitters."

"No," Sherri denied. "But I'm not about to be blindly led to the altar, either. I want to know what our plans are, and I think I have a right to ask."

Barrett shrugged. "What else is there to know? The wedding is all planned, small and simple, just like we both wanted. There'll be a small reception, and afterward we'll spend a week in Seattle for a honeymoon. Then we'll come back here, you can stay with my family while your hands get better, and I'll go to work. What other questions could you possibly have?"

Sherri studied him for a long moment. It all sounded very logical, but she wasn't satisfied. She had lived by her instincts for too many years to be thrown off the track now, and something was definitely wrong.

"You're lying to me," she said with certainty, not missing the small start he gave at her bald words. "I don't know why, but you are." Her throat constricted as Barrett drew near to take her in his arms.

"You want to call this off, don't you? Is that it?" she asked bravely. "For heaven's sake, Barrett, if you do, tell me to my face. I can take it," she lied.

She looked up at him, that dear, familiar face she had grown so used to seeing. "It . . . it isn't Karen, is it?"

Barrett's eyes narrowed with angry denial as he gently shook her. "No, you silly fool, why would I want her when I have you?"

"I don't know," Sherri said numbly. Her mind refused to accept what his words implied. "But something's wrong, I can tell," she insisted.

"Nothing's wrong," Barrett said vehemently. "Except that maybe I took too long to realize what you mean to me." He pulled her closer. "It's not to my credit that I never wanted you as my partner. And it's not to my credit that I did everything I could to keep from falling in love with you. But I have, thank God, and now that I have you, I'm never going to let you go. Do you hear me? Never!"

His lips covered hers with more than just passion. There was an intensity of emotion behind his embrace, and a rough stamp of ownership that had never been there before. Sherri welcomed it with ready lips and an open, welcoming heart. Her body shook with the evidence of his love, and she joyously returned measure for loving measure.

Barrett broke away first, his voice hoarse and trembling. "Forgive me, Sherri, but if I don't leave now, so help me I'll make love to you right here on my parents' parlor floor."

Sherri held on to him with a loving tenacity. "I wouldn't mind," she whispered. "But perhaps we should go upstairs?"

Barrett kissed her one more time. They supported each other all the way up the stairs, stopping every few steps to kiss again. By the time they reached Barrett's room, both of them were breathless with passion.

"You really love me?" Sherri asked as each undressed the other. Her happiness was a tangible thing, and it filled the darkened bedroom with a presence of its own.

"Let me show you," Barrett whispered, and he tenderly covered her body with his.

"Tell me," Sherri begged. "I've waited so long to hear you say the words." Her arms wound around him, holding him tight.

"I love you," he whispered in her ear, and Sherri smiled.

"Again," she urged, shivering with rapture as his hands began to do wonderful things to her.

"I love you," he whispered in her other ear, and Sherri's eyes closed briefly at the pleasure.

"Just once more," she pleaded, her heart soaring.

This time Barrett raised himself, his eyes open and inches away from hers. There was no mistaking the naked emotion in them. "I love you, Sherri Landers." His voice was serious, his words a solemn vow.

Only then could Sherri truly believe him. "You really do," she said with wonderment.

"I really do," he assured her, slowly stroking her hair. Then there were no more words, for words were no longer needed.

Much, much later, as they lay spent with passion in each other's arms, Sherri murmured quietly, "I never told you that I loved you."

Her eyes were shining in the darkness with a light of their own, and Barrett lovingly traced her eyebrows with a fingertip. "Oh, but you did," he contradicted as he pulled her even closer. "But I wouldn't mind hearing it again."

"I love you, too," Sherri answered, reaching for him as if she couldn't get enough of his touch. They cuddled in the dark in contented silence until Sherri again tried to bring up the subject that had been bothering her.

"Barrett . . ." she began, nestling her head against his shoulder.

"Hmmm?" he answered, pulling her closer.

"About my working... Does it really bother you so much?"

There was no answer, and for a moment Sherri thought that he had fallen asleep.

"Can't you understand my feelings?" he finally asked. "Look at it from a different point of view. Don't you also worry about me? Doesn't it bother you that my job involves risk, too?"

Sherri sighed. "Of course I worry about you. But I know that you're good at your job. I can't always look out for you, just as you can't always protect me. I trust you to take care of yourself, and I'd expect you to feel the same way about me."

"Very cleverly put," he answered unhappily.

"So you agree with me?"

Barrett refused to give her a direct answer. "You may not even be allowed back to work, Sherri, so if you don't mind, let's shelve the subject until we hear something definite."

Sherri had no choice but to acquiesce, for he gathered her roughly to him with a desperation that suddenly flamed into desire, thoroughly engulfing them both.

After that night most of the strain between them disappeared. True, Sherri still had a few lingering doubts about Barrett's acceptance of her intention to resume work, but just the sight of him was enough to push any uncertainty aside. For the first time, she began to feel excited about her upcoming wedding. Of course, compared to the night Barrett had declared his love for her, a wedding seemed somewhat anticlimatic. But it would mark an important turning point in her life, and she welcomed the security that a wedding ceremony would offer them both.

She didn't press Barrett any further regarding his plans for after the wedding. Her happiness was so complete that the news of his next position would only mean their separation, at least until she was working again, too. For the present, she was content to leave well enough alone.

THE WEDDING WAS NOW just days away. With Felicity's enthusiastic help, Sherri was planning her wardrobe for the honeymoon. Everyone else, including Barrett, had gone to the family's business office.

"This one looks nice." Felicity held a pale rose evening gown against her own tiny frame. "I'm so glad you decided to buy it."

Sherri agreed, although the price had been frightfully high. "I did need it," she said. "All my other clothes are still in Colorado."

The phone rang, and Felicity hurried to answer it. "It's for you," she announced, and Sherri frowned as she picked up the receiver. Who could be calling her?

It was the doctor's office in Portland. Sherri's appointment for tomorrow had to be canceled. Could she please come in today instead, more specifically, in half an hour?

"Just a minute," Sherri answered. She covered the mouthpiece with her hand as she explained the situation to Felicity. "Ordinarily I wouldn't mind missing one, but this was to be my last appointment before our honeymoon. Do you think you could drive me?"

"Of course," Felicity said instantly, and Sherri told the receptionist she would be there at the rescheduled time.

The waiting area of the doctor's office was crowded and there were no empty chairs. Felicity decided to go down to the hospital's cafeteria and have a cup of coffee, while Sherri found a vacant section of wall to lean against. She hoped she wouldn't have a long wait, but still, it was worth the inconvenience to keep her final appointment. She had worked hard at her exercises and she'd faithfully attended all her therapy sessions; now she wanted to hear the doctor's opinion before she went on her honeymoon.

Flexing her fingers, Sherri noted with satisfaction how much more easily they bent. And some of the scars seemed to be receding, too.

After only twenty minutes, the nurse called her name, and Sherri followed the woman into an examining room.

The doctor was prompt and thorough. After greeting her, he immediately started his examination of her hands, jotted down notes on her chart, then motioned Sherri into his office.

"You're doing very well," he told her. "I wish all my patients observed my instructions so diligently."

Sherri beamed with pleasure. "I have noticed an improvement. How soon do you think I can go back to work?"

"I beg your pardon?" The doctor gave her a strange look, and Sherri assumed he hadn't heard her properly.

"I asked when I could go back to work," she repeated.

The doctor removed his glasses. "Miss Landers, I was under the impression that you weren't going back to work."

Now it was Sherri's turn to look confused. "I always intended to return to my job," Sherri insisted. "Why would you think otherwise?"

The doctor turned the chart toward her so that she could read it. Attached were disability retirement papers filled out with her name, career history and medical statistics. Only her signature was missing.

"And who gave permission for these to be filled out?" she asked with deadly calm.

"Your fiancé, Mr. Barrett, did. He took care of all your paperwork while you were in the hospital. He had these drawn up by your employer in Denver, and of course they were forwarded to me," the doctor explained.

Sherri tried to ignore the angry roaring of emotion inside her head. "Did Mr. Barrett give you any reason why these papers weren't given to me to be signed?" Her hands clenched the leather of her purse so tightly she felt a surge of pain.

"Why yes, as a matter of fact, he did. He said there was no sense bothering you with these until after you were married. You would be changing your last name, and we'd just have to fill them out all over again so that your disability checks would carry your married name." The doctor took back the chart and closed it. "Obviously there's been some misunderstanding."

Now that was the understatement of the year, Sherri thought bitterly as she fought to keep her rage in check. How dare Barrett presume to make such a major decision in her life!

Sherri drew a deep breath. "Please destroy those papers, Doctor. And please write on my chart that I will not be retiring voluntarily. What's more, I intend to fight any mandatory retirement action that may be initiated against me."

The doctor nodded. "I'll certainly note those changes, Miss Landers."

"Thank you. And now I'd like to ask you again: when do you think I'll be certified fit for duty?"

The doctor shook his head. "I really can't say. You've made a remarkable recovery, considering the damage sustained by your hands during the initial injury. In fact, you've done so well that I've decided to release you from any further treatment. There's nothing more we can do for you here.

"You see," he continued, "Your condition is such that while I couldn't certify you unfit for duty, I couldn't in all conscience say that you're completely fit, either. There's no denying that you'll have permanent damage to those hands. Any kind of work requiring fine motion, like painting or playing a musical instrument, or even prolonged writing, will be difficult if not impossible for you."

Sherri sighed with frustration. "So where does that leave me?"

"In my experience, it's usually up to the employee to prove his or her fitness for duty. If your intention was to stay with the forest rangers, you should never have left Colorado and your old employer. It's established procedure, Miss Landers. I thought you knew."

"No, I didn't know," Sherri told him. But Barrett did, of that she was certain, and he had deliberately taken her away.

"Is there anything else?" the doctor asked, breaking into Sherri's frantic thoughts.

"Yes. You can send my medical records back to Denver." She stood up and clutched the back of her chair for support against the crumbling of her world. "I'm going home."

SHERRI PACKED IN THE SILENCE of the late afternoon. On the way home, she'd been so obviously distressed that Felicity had become concerned, though Sherri refused to answer any questions. The younger woman had wanted to accompany her upstairs to her room, but Sherri had curtly, almost rudely, refused.

Felicity left, full of determination, and Sherri was sure she'd go straight to Barrett, who would of course come rushing home to check on her. Well, let him come, Sherri thought angrily as she folded the new clothes she had bought for her honeymoon. She wanted to hear his side of the story, but she feared already that it could make no difference to her decision.

A knock at the door heralded Barrett's arrival.

"Sherri, may I come in?" He didn't wait for an answer, but opened the door and stood just inside the room.

"My sister said you weren't feeling well, so I thought—" At the sight of her open suitcase, he broke off abruptly, his hand motionless on the doorknob.

"What is going on?" he asked hoarsely.

"Close the door, please," Sherri requested. Barrett seemed frozen in place, and Sherri was suddenly reminded of a stag staring at the weapon that would finish him. Her heart twisted at his pain, but she was determined to have her say.

"I'd like to postpone the wedding," she said clearly. Barrett finally moved then, closing the door and dropping into the nearest chair.

"It's in two days!" he protested, his face rigid with shock. "What is so important that it can't wait two days?"

Sherri continued to pack, for she couldn't bring herself to confront the despair in his eyes.

"Did Felicity tell you that my doctor's appointment was rescheduled? I've just come back from there." She folded and refolded the same blouse, then went on in a quiet voice. "I found out about my supposed retirement plans, Barrett. And I'm not happy about them at all."

"I see," Barrett said, sounding almost relieved. Some of the agitation disappeared from his manner. "Sherri, I can explain."

Sherri turned around to face him, then sat down on the bed, the open suitcase a stark barrier between them.

"Please do."

Barrett hesitated, as if he didn't know how to start. "You were so very sick at first, Sherri. None of us thought you'd get well enough to go back to work. It was only logical for us to fill out those papers."

"That was at first, Barrett. I'm not that sick now. In fact, the doctor said I was finished with my treatments."

"Did he say you were fit to go back to work?" he asked tensely.

"No," she admitted.

"I knew it," was his triumphant reply, but Sherri hadn't finished.

"He didn't say that I couldn't, either. I do have to prove my fitness for duty to Holden, back in Colorado, but you knew that all along. That's why you dragged me here to Portland, isn't it?"

Barrett shrugged. "It was for your own good."

"How dare you make that decision for me!" Sherri's hands clenched with resentment. "My job is my life!"

"I thought I was," came his anguished reply. Barrett turned away from her, his eyes filled with pain.

"Oh, Barrett... You *are* my life, you always will be," Sherri proclaimed. "You know that. But what am I supposed to do while you're off at work? I'm not trained for anything else, and damn it, Barrett, I don't *want* to do anything else! I'm good at my job. What do you want me to do? Sit at home in an empty house waiting for you? And only come to life when you're home on weekends? Is that what you want for me?''

Barrett refused to answer her question. "You could get hurt again, Sherri. You aren't fit enough to be a ranger now, and you weren't fit to be one before, or you wouldn't have hurt yourself in the first place," he said callously.

"Tell that to all the people I've helped," was Sherri's stinging reply. "I'm going back to Colorado. I'm going to fight for my job, and I'm going to get it back. Then, and only then, will I marry you."

Barrett rose from his chair to grasp her by the arms. "I thought you loved me," he pleaded. "I can't believe this is happening. And for the second time, no less. First Karen, now you." His face was pale beneath the shocked green eyes.

Sherri hardened herself against his agony and her own as she gently pushed him away. "I love you, Miles Barrett," she whispered. "You'll never know how much. But you can't truly love me in return if you want me to spend my life on a shelf. Looking back, I can see that your attitude has gone from bad to worse! On our first assignment together you chased away that couple who gave us an unfriendly send-off. Then you ate all your meals with me when the rumors about us started, so that I wouldn't hear them."

"Was that so terribly wrong?" he demanded.

"Not what you did—but *why*. I have to admit that with one part of me, I did appreciate your efforts to protect me, but that's not a feeling I'm proud of. I don't want to be protected from life, not even from pain! What about when you wanted to haul me up out of the ravine instead of letting me climb out? You wanted to risk your own life—and the lives of those two boys—because you didn't trust my instincts and my skills. I had to yank the rope down out of your reach to guarantee your safety! And what about now, Barrett? What about my job? You made a decision about *my* life *without even consulting me,*" she continued mercilessly. "Don't I get some say in the matter?"

She took a deep, steadying breath. "You're wrong, Barrett, and you refuse to admit it! I would never even consider dictating to you about your job, yet you refuse to allow me that same right. I don't want to be protected from the world on the chance that I might get hurt. Don't you want me to be happy and fulfilled?"

"You don't need your job for that," Barrett stubbornly insisted. "I can do that for you."

"No, you can't," Sherri said. "You can't, because you don't trust me. You didn't trust me as your partner, and you wouldn't trust me as your wife. You think my decisions aren't reliable! You're intending to make them all for me to preserve your own peace of mind! I refuse to walk into marriage with a man who doesn't allow me to stand on my own two feet."

Sherri turned decisively away from him. "I deserve more. And so do you." She grabbed up the rest of her pile of unpacked clothes and roughly dumped them all into the suitcase.

"I'm ready to go," she announced, her eyes large and dark in her pale face. "Will you drive me to the airport?"

"Find your own ride." He fell wearily back into the chair. "I suppose I should thank you for breaking it off with me in person," he added with bitterness. "Karen only sent me a letter."

"Oh, Barrett . . ." Sherri sighed. The comparison wounded her, as he had known it would. "I'm not breaking anything off. I'm just postponing things for a while, that's all. My job won't wait forever."

"Don't do this to us," Barrett pleaded in a ghost of his usual robust voice.

Sherri gathered up her purse and her jacket. "I'm only postponing a marriage ceremony. That isn't anywhere near as bad as your deceiving me and deliberately plotting to take my job away from me. I can understand your motives, but I can't possibly agree with them.

"Please, Barrett, come with me!" she suddenly begged. "We can work this out, I know we can."

Barrett shook his head. "No. I refuse to go back and watch you get yourself killed. I'd do anything for you, Sherri, anything at all, but not that. Not that," he repeated dully.

"How many times must I tell you that I can be trusted to take care of myself?" Sherri cried out. "Barrett, I want to keep my job, and that means I have to leave. Come back with me," she begged again, her eyes spilling over with tears as she reached for his hands.

Barrett refused to rise from the chair. "No," he declared, and Sherri's heart shriveled at the finality in his voice.

"Will you stay and marry me?" he asked one last time, his body tensing as he waited for her answer.

Sherri thought about life without him, and she almost wavered. Not to see him again! Not to hear the drawling voice that disguised a heart as big as the outdoors. Not to have him hold her in his arms again, bringing her body to that sweet fever pitch . . . She couldn't possibly bear it.

"Sherri?" came the uncertain query.

Sherri blinked, realizing that she'd closed her eyes. She focused on him again. All she had to do was say "I'll stay," and both of them would be spared irrevocable pain. But the Sherri Landers she knew would be irrevocably lost.

"I can't," she whispered. Her horrified eyes watched as the man she loved changed into an unrecognizable stranger who walked silently out of the room.

# CHAPTER NINE

THAT WAS THE LAST Sherri saw of Barrett before Felicity drove her to the airport. Sherri had painfully explained her reasons for leaving to the whole family, being careful not to place any blame on Barrett. She did ask that they console him as best they could and try to forgive her for causing so much trouble after all their kindness. Afraid of breaking down in tears, she didn't dare tell them that she would be waiting for Barrett if he changed his mind. Sherri wasn't aware that her visible suffering told the truth more effectively than any words could have done. And so she left, all the while vainly hoping for one last glimpse of Barrett before she boarded the plane to Denver.

As always, winter had come early to the high country of Colorado. The snow-covered mountains glittered with a savage, lonely beauty beneath the wings of the small plane that was taking her back to the ranger station. But it was only the loneliness that spoke to Sherri now. The starkness of the landscape seemed to mock her, and she closed her eyes in despair, refusing to look out the window.

After filling out the necessary paperwork in Denver, Sherri had called Holden to let him know she was coming back. She returned to find the compound deep in snow, the temperature bitterly cold. It felt strange to be walking past her old quarters at the ranger station and up the stairs to Holden's office. It was more than strange to go by Barrett's empty cabin. It was heart-wrenching.

Sherri sat stiffly while Holden reviewed her medical papers, gazing out the windows and wondering how much longer she'd be forced to wait there in silence. Patience didn't seem to be her strong suit lately.

"Hmm." Holden laid her file aside. "I've just read the official version. Now let's hear your side of the story." He leaned back in his chair, the thick fingers reaching for a cigar.

"I want to come back, sir," Sherri said simply.

"That isn't what I heard. I thought you and Barrett were planning to live happily ever after, and that you were becoming a lady of leisure." His next words were blunt. "I don't have time for a ranger who can't make up her mind." He blew a noxious cloud of cigar smoke into the air.

"I always wanted to come back," Sherri insisted. "Barrett thought that I—" She broke off and started again. "There was a misunderstanding," she settled for saying.

Holden studied her for a long silent moment. "I believe you, Landers," he finally said. "I never took you for a quitter." He puffed on his cigar several times, then asked, "Am I correct in assuming that your marriage is off?"

Sherri nodded, trying not to let her misery show.

"You realize, don't you, that Barrett will be coming back here?" Holden asked. "Your marriage was the only reason he was granted a transfer. It will soon be revoked, if it hasn't been already. Can you handle working with him again?"

"If you're taking me back, I can handle anything," Sherri answered with determination. Holden couldn't know her sudden rise in spirits was due to the prospect of seeing Barrett again.

"I'm taking you back on a trial basis only," Holden said, dampening her spirits. "For a while you'll be on limited duties, such as office work and training the new rangers. Gradually I'll work you up to more strenuous tasks. If your endurance and physical stamina are acceptable, and if you don't reveal any psychological problems—"

"Psychological problems, sir?" Sherri broke in abruptly, though she intended no rudeness.

Holden neatly flicked a cylinder of ash into his ashtray. "What if there's a rescue during a fire? What if I send you, and you go to pieces? What if someone dies because you panic?" He stabbed the cigar in the direction of her hands.

"That would never happen!" Sherri was horrified at the mere thought.

Holden shrugged. "So you say. But I'll want to see for myself. And you understand, of course, that if I'm not satisfied with any aspect of your performance, you're gone."

Sherri unconsciously clenched her hands into fists, as if to ward off his threats. "I understand."

"Your old quarters are still available," Holden informed her. "Please report to the office first thing in the morning. You're on phone duty."

"Thank you, sir." Sherri rose and put on her coat in preparation for the cold walk to her quarters.

Holden studied her thoughtfully, then said in his blunt fashion, "Frankly, Landers, I never believed the two of you would ever make it to the altar. Barrett isn't any woman's dream. Don't you think you're better off without him?"

Resentment at Holden's words flared through Sherri as she finished fastening her coat. She opened her mouth to contradict him, then suddenly paused. How could she argue with her superior when she had asked herself that very question?

"You wished to say something?" Holden asked keenly.

Sherri shook her head in dejection, then left the room, all the while feeling Holden's eyes on her back.

Later she condemned herself for not standing up to him, and vowed that next time she would be more outspoken in Barrett's defense. However, she wouldn't raise the subject herself, and nothing more was ever said by Holden.

And so her routine began. Phone duties, scheduling duties, filing duties, any dull job that came into Holden's office was automatically hers. Sherri hated it, but recognized the caution behind Holden's actions. She did as she was told, didn't complain, and tried desperately to occupy her mind with work to avoid thinking of Barrett.

Her roommate, Janet, was away on a vacation, so Sherri had their cabin to herself. She'd expected to spend all her evenings alone, but much to her surprise she had frequent visitors. No one except Barrett had seen her since the fire and her hospitalization, and it soon became apparent that most of the camp's staff was making a point of checking up on her. Many of her fellow rangers offered not only their concern, but their friendship.

Acknowledgment by her peers was something she had always been denied, and at one time Sherri would have welcomed her newfound popularity with open arms. Now, however, it meant very little. The face behind every knock on her door was never the face she yearned to see; in spite of herself, she couldn't become resigned to the disappointment she felt each time it was someone else.

Finally she took to avoiding her cabin altogether during her free time. She would ride her horses, alternating between the mare and the gelding to ensure that they both got plenty of much-needed exercise. And her long rambles on horseback also ensured that she was left alone with the beauty of the mountains. More than anything else, their familiar serenity helped to soothe her broken spirit.

Every day Sherri searched eagerly through the paperwork that was now her full-time job for news of Barrett's return. She found no indication of his arrival date, though, and her pride wouldn't allow her to ask Holden for any information. However, working in Holden's office had some advantages. Sherri took the opportunity to borrow a duplicate key to Barrett's cabin, determined to see if his gear had been shipped on ahead, because she was frantic for news of him.

Her first visit proved to be a disappointment, and against her better judgment, Sherri established a daily routine of visiting his cabin. Each day after her shift, she would check for any sign of Barrett's return. When she discovered that everything was still the same, untouched from the day before, she would linger in the cabin, dusting the furniture and briefly airing out the rooms. Once in a while she would find herself opening his closet to breathe in the faint scent of Barrett that gently wafted out. She'd close her eyes and pretend that he was there beside her, but the fantasy never offered more than a few seconds of pleasure before reality once again set in.

"I wish I'd never met him," she said vehemently. "Never, never, never!" and she slammed the closet door shut with a bang. But she couldn't truly mean the words.

She had been back at the camp for about a month when Holden asked her, one afternoon, if she could work some extra hours. He had a quarterly report to finish and desperately needed her help. Sherri instantly agreed, for anything was better than wandering aimlessly around Barrett's rooms for the rest of the evening. When she finally left the office, it was dark outside, but she glanced automatically in the direction of his cabin. A light was clearly visible.

Sherri's heart leaped with excitement. She dashed across the compound and hurriedly inserted her key in the lock with shaking hands.

"Barrett? Barrett, you're back!" she gasped at the sight of him, more breathless from excitement than from running.

"Would you close the door, please? It's below freezing outside," came the polite, impassive answer.

The smile fell from Sherri's face as she complied. His expression was as distant and unwelcoming as his words.

"What are you doing here?" He was sitting on the sofa and pointedly refused to offer her a seat.

"I...I let myself in. I have a key," she stammered, standing awkwardly just inside the door.

"I can see that. As I don't remember giving you one, I can only assume you stole this one from Holden's office." Barrett paused. "I'd appreciate having it returned. I don't like trespassers in my room."

Sherri bit her lip, determined not to show how much he was hurting her. "I merely dusted and aired the cabin a few times. I'm sorry if that offends you."

That drew an immediate reaction from Barrett. "You had your chance to play housewife when I asked you to marry me. Considering that you couldn't wait to leave Portland, I hardly think your domestic contributions are appropriate."

"Sarcasm doesn't become you, Barrett," Sherri said unhappily.

"Neither does being stood up at the altar," he replied, rising to his feet to pace the room.

"Do you realize how hurt my family was by your escape act? Not to mention my own feelings, of course."

"And what about mine?" Sherri responded with quiet calm. If only she could make him see things from her point of view. "Barrett, I would have married you instantly if you'd only said three words to me."

"'I love you?'" he asked bitterly. "I seem to remember saying them more than once."

"I know, and I remember each and every time," she said, swallowing down the lump in her throat. "But what I really want you to say is 'I trust you.' I want you to let me make my own decisions regarding my life, and that includes my job. I want you to stop hovering over me like some protective mother hen!" Sherri insisted. "You never used to do that before."

"You were just another ranger then. I didn't care about you before!" He sank back onto the sofa and ran his hands distractedly through his hair. "Sherri, it drives me crazy, thinking of you getting hurt again. I can't sleep, I can't eat, I—" He stopped and swallowed hard, and allowed Sherri to gently sink down beside him.

"I just want to protect you! That's what a man is supposed to do for the woman he loves. I'm not wrong, damn it, I'm not!" he shouted as he raised his head to defy her with glittering eyes.

Sherri's own eyes flashed with anger. "Does your love mean lying to me? You didn't let me know that I didn't have to retire. You took me away from here without telling me that I could lose my job as a consequence. You insulted me by saying that my injuries were the result of my incompetence. And all along, what you really wanted was for me to hide myself away in some safe little hole. Barrett, that isn't love!" Sherri insisted mercilessly, although her heart was breaking at his pain.

Barrett turned pale at her words. "Are you saying you don't believe I love you?" he asked hoarsely.

Sherri reached to touch him, to comfort, but he recoiled as though she'd struck him.

"Don't you touch me," he hissed, with such venom that Sherri's hand froze in midair.

"Congratulations, my dear, on delivering the ultimate insult." Barrett's face was still pale, but the old arrogant tone was back, and too late Sherri realized that she had gone too far.

"Maybe you're right." He rose from the chair, and then roughly pulled her to her feet and pushed her toward the door. "Maybe I don't love you. You're just some biological disease I've caught, like a fever. Well, I can get over you. I got over Karen, and that should give me plenty of experience for the second time around."

"Barrett," Sherri pleaded, aghast at the masklike hardness of his face.

"I'm quitting you cold, Landers. From now on you don't exist. Do you hear me, ex-partner? I can only hope you enjoy your new life as Holden's girl Friday. Maybe he can provide the distractions you need to give your life some excitement, because you sure as hell won't be getting anything more from me!"

Sherri's stomach twisted at his viciousness, and she grabbed the doorjamb to steady herself. Her eyes filled, and the tears overflowed and ran down her cheeks. Barrett turned his back on her, as though he were afraid the sight of her would weaken his resolve.

"Please go," he ordered, still refusing to look at her.

Sherri dashed a hand across her wet face. "I'm sorry," she choked out. "I won't be bothering you again."

FROM THEN ON BARRETT ACTED as though Sherri didn't even exist. Not a word or a glance did he direct her way, and Sherri died inside each time she saw him. She'd made her position clear, and right or wrong, Barrett intended to see that she lived by it.

She had too much pride to show the rest of the camp how shattered she was. With dogged determination, she worked as hard and as thoroughly at her office tasks as she had on her field jobs. Although her dedication didn't lessen her heartache, she gradually found it easier to maintain a calm exterior among her co-workers. And one by one, the days passed with lonely, monotonous regularity, until the first missing person of the winter was radioed in.

Holden had taken the call while Sherri was at lunch, and he'd immediately sent out five teams. When Sherri returned, those teams were already in the field, and Sherri sighed with disappointment. Although she hadn't once asked Holden for an outdoor assignment, she would have pressed him for this one. It was the kind of rescue she excelled at. She knew that her tracking skills and familiarity with the terrain would have been a definite advantage; the general location of the missing adult male was sketchy, the man's description was hazy, and worse yet, it had started to snow.

Sherri had to settle for operating the radio and keeping tabs on the search teams. The five teams were good, she noted. All were experienced rangers, and she had trained two of the teams herself. Still, they hadn't found any sign of the man yet.

The snow continued to fall in big, cottony chunks. It was not a true blizzard, for there was very little wind, but the snow fell hard and heavy just the same. Visibility was next to nothing, and Sherri waited anxiously for the last rescue team to return. All the others had been forced to abandon the search for the missing man, and Sherri knew by the radio's continued silence that the last team had failed, too.

"Here they come now," Holden muttered with relief. The snowstorm was expected to last throughout the night. It would be dark soon, which meant no further search efforts could be made today.

"Did you find him?" Sherri asked urgently as one half of the remaining team came inside the command post.

Jerry Myers shook his head. He was covered with snow, his face bloodless from the cold. "We didn't even find a trace. My partner's at the aid station, sir," Myers informed Holden. "I think she has frostbite."

Holden sighed. "You both did what you could," he consoled the ranger. "You tell your partner that. You probably shouldn't even have stayed out as long as you did. You did everything you could," he repeated. But disappointment filled the room.

"I'm calling off the search for the night," Holden announced reluctantly. "Why don't you turn in, Myers? You look beat."

Myers nodded. "We really tried, sir," he said in a hoarse, defeated voice.

Holden watched him leave, then viciously stabbed out his cigar. "If only we could have used the helicopters! But with this storm, well, the poor fool's probably dead by now. How could anyone be stupid enough to go cross-country skiing alone in this wilderness?"

Sherri froze in her seat. "You didn't tell me he was skiing cross-country! I thought he was a hiker!" she burst out.

"What difference would it make, Landers? You weren't assigned to a search-and-rescue team."

"But I know where he is!" Sherri exclaimed. "Or at least I have a good idea where to look. The time we've wasted, sir! There's only one place around here where anyone could cross-country ski!"

"Don't be ridiculous, Landers," Holden scoffed. "There's no such place around here."

"But there is!" Sherri insisted. "You have to let me go out there!"

"You're still on limited duty, Landers. I'm going to have to refuse your request." He watched her with a calculating expression, then turned his attention to the work on his desk. "Of course, what you do with your free time is your own business," he said in an offhand voice.

Sherri pushed away from her desk. "Are you saying what I think you're saying?" she asked incredulously. Holden's face was blandly innocent, and Sherri's brain took a few seconds to grasp the situation.

"Oh ... I see," she slowly realized. "You don't want to take responsibility for sending me out, do you? If I fail, you'd have to take the blame for giving a ranger on limited duty your official permission. But if I go on my own, you're in the clear. And if I succeed, so much the better."

"I didn't mean that at all," Holden denied, but both he and Sherri knew otherwise. "Regulations are regulations, as you well know," he continued. "But if you're serious about returning to full duty, you shouldn't be averse to contributing a little of your free time to proving it."

Sherri reached for her coat. She knew he was giving her the chance she had patiently waited for, yet she was angry at the way he'd chosen to do it.

"After all the assignments and rescues I've handled successfully, why must I continue to prove myself?" she demanded.

"You don't, Sherri. Not to me, at least," came a third voice, and Sherri whirled around to see Barrett standing in the doorway.

"I'd like to volunteer to go along with Landers." Barrett's eyes were full of anger at Holden. He crossed the room to help a stunned Sherri on with her coat.

"As I've already explained to Sherri, what you rangers do with your free time is your own business," Holden repeated calmly.

Barrett gave his boss a look of scorn, then turned toward Sherri. "I've already packed our gear. I'll go and saddle the horses while you change into your warmest clothes. And I'll clear up this paperwork for you. Get going, Landers."

He gently pushed Sherri in the direction of the door, then sat down at her desk. He acted as though Holden weren't even in the room. Sherri paused, leaning against the doorjamb to support her shaking legs. She took in Barrett's broad form with greedy eyes, her heart thrilling to the sound of his voice. He was actually speaking to her again! How had he known she was leaving to search for the skier on her own? And what had made him decide to go with her? Whatever the reason, she was thankful for his presence. Like her, he placed the value of a human life above everything; like her, he was willing to risk his own in the attempt to save a stranger. She had never loved Barrett more than at this moment.

"Best hurry," he urged without looking up. "Every minute counts."

The familiar surge of adrenaline flooded through her veins, and she was off, completely missing Holden's satisfied smile as he watched her leave.

THE SNOW CONTINUED TO FALL as Sherri led the way on the mare. The whitened branches of the trees were bent unnaturally close to the ground, and the occasional sudden cracking as they snapped under the snow's weight was the only sound other than the plodding of the horses.

"Where are we headed?" Barrett asked when they'd left the ranger station far behind.

Sherri slowed the mare and allowed him to catch up to her on the gelding. "About thirty miles from here there's a large break in the granite on one of the slopes. It makes a natural trail and continues on for about three miles. If he was cross-country skiing anywhere, it would have to be there."

The horses lurched and stumbled through a drift that reached their underbellies, and both riders had to concentrate on keeping their seats. When they were clear of the drift, Barrett spoke again. "I know that area, and Sherri, the other teams have already searched there. Holden did an excellent job of positioning everyone. We're just going to be covering the same ground."

"They didn't know where to look." Sherri brushed away the snow that was sticking to her eyelashes. "There are some deep fissures in that granite trail. They aren't very wide, but they're wide enough for a man to fall into. The snow would have drifted into them much earlier. If that skier's anywhere, he's in one of those fissures."

"No. Oh, no," was Barrett's agonized outburst, and Sherri instantly understood the reason for it. If she was correct in her assumptions, then this rescue could actually turn into a nightmarish replay of their last one.

The quiet of the night continued unbroken except for the labored breathing of the horses as they struggled through the depths of snow. But it was fairly shallow in one open, sweeping expanse; there, they could ride abreast, and talking was easier.

"Barrett... How did you know I was leaving to search on my own?" Sherri asked, gazing across at him in the failing light. What little sunlight remained, filtering through the heavy cloud cover, would soon be gone. "I didn't even know that the missing man was on skis until just before you showed up."

"I don't know," he answered slowly. "I was alone in my cabin, and suddenly I had the strangest feeling that you were leaving the camp. I couldn't possibly let you go out into this alone, so I packed up our gear, and went to look for you." He shook his head in puzzlement. "I can't really explain it."

Sherri took his words and gathered them to her heart. So he still felt some emotional link to her, however hard he had tried to break it.

"I'm glad you're here," she said after a moment. "If I'm right about what's ahead, I'll certainly need your help."

Barrett frowned at that. "Damn it, Sherri, why didn't you tell me about those fissures?" he asked. The snow covered his shoulders, hat and back, and he impatiently brushed at his face.

"Would you have let me come out here if I had?" she countered. There was no answer to her question, and Sherri exhaled with annoyance. "It's the same old story, isn't it? You don't trust me to take care of myself."

"Look at your hands!" Barrett exclaimed.

"It was just one time, Barrett, just one time! Risks are part of this job! How can you have been a ranger for three years and not learned that? Do you think *you're* invincible?"

"Not where you're concerned," he mumbled under his breath, but she didn't hear his words.

Darkness fell, and Sherri checked her surroundings again. They had barely covered ten miles after all this time. She thought of the missing skier lost and alone, out in this weather. The night would be half over before they even got close to their destination. Still, they had a few things in their favor. There was almost no wind, and it wasn't bitterly cold. The damp, clumpy snowfall was evidence that the temperature had risen above the freezing point. And best of all, there was a full moon. From time to time it would emerge from among the clouds to cast its weak light on the reflective surface of the snow. It wasn't much, but it was enough to give Sherri her bearings.

"Do you want to stop for a quick coffee? I brought along a thermos," Barrett said from behind. His voice was muffled in the snow-filled air.

"Only if you're cold and you need it," Sherri answered. She turned around in her saddle to face him. "I'm fine, myself, and I'd rather push on. We're still only halfway there."

Barrett thought of the missing man and gloomily shook his head, then checked his compass. "How do you ever manage to find your way in this?" he asked with admiring disbelief. His compass showed her path to be true, without needless deviations. Until he read the compass, he'd had no idea of their direction; they could have been going around in circles for all he knew.

"My father always told me it was a gift." Sherri smiled at the memory. "He had it, too, so I suppose I inherited it. I don't think I've used my compass from the day I was issued it." She clicked her tongue to the mare, and they were moving again.

"But you do carry one, don't you?" Barrett asked.

"Of course. It's regulations." Sherri missed the half-tender, half-exasperated look he gave her.

The snow continued to fall, and the night wore on. From time to time Sherri would lean forward and rest her frozen face on Ladybug's neck. The mare was used to such unorthodox treatment, and plodded steadily on with the persistence of her mustang breeding. Sherri turned around to catch Barrett following her example.

"Why don't you grow a beard?" she asked him.

He pulled off a glove and rubbed at his cheeks with warm fingers. "I don't know. I've never had one before. Do you think you'd like it?"

Sherri's eyes were intent on his face. "I didn't think my opinion mattered to you anymore." Her words floated softly in the air, and Barrett had to strain to hear her.

"It matters," he said simply. He pulled on his glove and concentrated on his riding again.

Sherri knew his gaze was on her, its electricity as easy to feel as the cold of the night. But she said nothing. The fact that he could admit she still mattered to him was more than enough for now.

The horses were breathing heavily, their breath a white mist above their flaring nostrils, when Sherri pulled Ladybug to a halt. "We're here," she announced.

Trusting her judgment, Barrett didn't even bother to check his compass. He immediately stopped and reached for his snowshoes. It was only when they both had their snowshoes on that they dismounted.

"You're the first person I've ever met, besides my father and me, who puts on snowshoes before getting out of the saddle," Sherri marveled as she tied the mare's reins to a tree.

Barrett tossed her his old superior look. "I have no intention of sinking into all that snow when I can stay perfectly dry." He unfastened the rescue ropes from his saddle, while Sherri got the first-aid kit and the flashlights from hers.

"We need a long stick, Barrett," she called out, but a quick glance showed her that he was already carrying one. At her bossiness, his eyes narrowed in mocking reproach, and Sherri almost smiled.

"Sorry. Habit." She checked her bearings again, then waited for more light from the moon to make certain of her location. Those fissures were deep.

"All set?" Barrett asked, and Sherri nodded. "And you don't have to remind me to stay close," he added. "Just consider me your shadow."

"That ledge slopes downward from northwest to southeast, Barrett," Sherri panted out as she half walked, half ran, in the peculiar gait required by snowshoes.

"Are we headed for the west end first? That's where that skier would have started," Barrett surmised. "Let's hope he wasn't stupid enough to ski uphill all the way and start at the east end," Barrett said angrily.

They'd covered about twenty yards when Sherri stopped. "The snow! Is it me, or is it starting to let up?"

"It's been tapering off the past fifteen minutes. You're slipping, partner," Barrett chided, but Sherri just grinned and didn't answer. This was the Barrett she knew and loved.

She slowly approached the granite slope, parts of the jagged rock shining bare in the moonlight.

"That first fissure should be right about here."

Barrett instantly threw out his arm in a protective gesture meant to keep her from advancing. He started probing with the stick. Five feet in front of them the stick sank as far as Barrett's hand.

"Cutting it awfully close, aren't we, Landers?" He carefully studied the snow. "I don't see any sign of an accident. The snow is perfectly smooth."

Sherri nodded in agreement. Even if they were wrong and the skier was beneath them, their mission was over. Anyone under the weight of all that snow was beyond rescue.

She paused, considering. She was trying to picture the fissures. One in particular leaped into her mind. About fifteen feet deep, it was sheltered under a rocky outcropping, so not only would it be relatively free of snow and therefore easy to check, it would also be hidden in shadow—hidden enough so that an unwary skier might not see it until the last minute.

"Come on," she urged excitedly. "I think I have a good idea where this guy is."

Sherri swung a wide arc around the other dangerous areas and aimed for a spot to the right and downhill. The rocky outcropping was easily visible, as were the faint grooves in the snow. Parallel grooves that were almost, but not quite, filled in.

Her eyes sparkled as she saw Barrett instantly notice the ski grooves himself. He looked at her in open admiration. "You're right on the mark, lady."

Sherri glowed with pleasure, but wasted no time basking in his praise. "Let's hope this poor fool is still breathing," she prayed.

They cautiously approached the fissure. Now Barrett led the way, and Sherri felt her palms begin to sweat in spite of the cold as she peered over the edge.

"Nothing!" She could have cried with disappointment. "I was sure he was here!" she wailed. Could they have wasted the whole night searching in the wrong area?

"No, wait, I see something!" Barrett was shining his light into the near, more exposed corner of the crevice where some snow had fallen. "See? Look!" The light revealed a faint streak of vivid red—a red that wasn't found in nature. "He's in there, Sherri."

Sherri wasn't ready to heave a sigh of relief quite yet. Adding her light to Barrett's, she saw that the man was facedown and almost completely covered in snow. She desperately hoped he hadn't suffocated.

They both eased back from the edge. "Plan of action?" Sherri asked.

"I didn't think my opinions mattered anymore," Barrett echoed her earlier words. "At least where your almighty job is concerned." A trace of the old bitterness still remained.

"Everything about you matters to me, Barrett. It always has." Sherri's love was visible in her eyes, and she made no attempt to hide her longing for him.

Barrett gave her a piercing look, then directed his attention to the job at hand.

"We can get the horses in here, can't we?" he asked. "We'll need their strength. There's no place to rig up a block and tackle for our pulleys, and with this snow there's not enough traction for me to do a brute-strength haul."

"We can get them in," Sherri agreed. "Do you want to lower me down first while you go get the horses? I can work on him to save time."

"No!" was his vehement answer, and Sherri's heart sank. Was he remembering the fire-filled ravine? Was he going to insist on sheltering her again?

"You'd better wait until I get back, Sherri. If anything happens to me, you'll be stuck down there alone. This guy's been here for so long that another few minutes couldn't possibly make much difference."

"You don't know that," Sherri told him, but she saw the wisdom of his words.

"Besides, there's more. Look up, love." The endearment slipped out as Barrett pointed upward.

The rocky outcropping was blanketed with a massive covering of snow. The steepness of the incline meant that the heavier the snow layer became, the more likely it was to slide off. Sherri followed its theoretic path. It would fall right into the fissure, easily filling the bottom half of the hole. She shivered violently.

"Didn't see that, did you?" Barrett said softly. "I know you want to get this guy out. So do I, but sometimes you have to stand back from your emotions to take stock." His words hinted at a double meaning, and his eyes held hers tenaciously.

"So, shall we both go get the horses? Then, you can go down when we return, after—and only after—you're harnessed to the horses. I don't like the looks of that." He tossed his head upward. "Agreed?"

"Agreed." Sherri slowly backed away from the looming shadow of the outcropping. She began to say the same prayer she said on every rescue. *Please, dear Lord, make this guy be all right.* Then she added, *And make things right for me and Barrett, too.*

As they laboriously snowshoed back to the horses, Sherri suddenly realized that the wind had started rising steadily; she'd been too preoccupied to notice before. Brownie was acting up; the sound of the wind must have made him nervous. Sherri watched Barrett calmly settle him. He had a way with the gelding that she'd never had, and she was grateful now instead of jealous. A loud noise could send that damp, heavy snow crashing onto the skier or herself. Or Barrett. She flinched with horror at the thought. Barrett saw her agitation, rode up beside her and grabbed her arm.

"You okay?" he asked with concern.

"You keep that horse quiet near that outcropping, or so help me, he goes to the auction block," were her cruel words, but Barrett understood the worry that prompted them.

"Nothing's going to happen to me, Sherri. And I promise nothing is going to happen to you, either," he said calmly. Sherri tried to relax a little.

"We should have radioed in as soon as we found him," she fretted.

"I didn't forget," Barrett replied. "They can't get a chopper up in this wind, and requesting a chopper is the only reason I would have called in. I intend to let Holden sweat out our positions until the last possible second," Barrett vowed. "I can't believe he refused to officially stand behind you."

"He's giving me a chance to prove myself the only way he can." Sherri defended Holden, hoping to defuse Barrett's anger.

"Some chance. He gave you about as much of a chance as I did." Barrett swallowed hard, and concentrated on brushing the snow off the gelding's neck.

She wished they could follow this conversational track at their leisure, but it would have to wait until the rescue was completed. "Barrett, we've got to call in the coordinates, for our own safety if nothing else," she insisted. "If you don't do it, I will."

Barrett sighed heavily and prepared to make radio contact with the station, as Sherri stood quietly by. He relayed the information in a brusque, impatient tone, then signed off abruptly. Spurring his horse forward, he grabbed on to the saddle horn as Brownie tripped and scrambled for a foothold inside another drift.

Sherri immediately moved to catch up to him, but the mare was smaller and had trouble negotiating the drift Brownie and Barrett had cleared. Sherri murmured encouragement, and eventually they emerged. She moved the mare as close as she could to the gelding.

"Barrett..." She started to say, "Please don't shut me out!" but the silhouette of the outcropping loomed before her. Her urge to talk to him about personal matters had to be put aside until later. They had important work to do, and every second counted.

Not long afterward, Barrett was checking and double-checking the harness around Sherri's waist. He nodded, satisfied that it was secure. He took her cold face between his gloved hands and kissed her hard on the mouth.

"That's for luck," he told her. "Ready, partner?"

Sherri refused to allow herself to look up at that massive weight of snow. She tightly closed both hands over the rope to anchor herself. They remained somewhat stiff, but they were strong, and they hadn't yet begun to hurt.

"Ready," she answered.

"Good girl. Here we go."

The darkness of the night changed to the even blacker darkness of the fissure as Sherri descended. She could hear the sounds of the horses' efforts echoing eerily off the walls. At least this was no ravine. She should be touching bottom any second now.

"Okay!" she called. "I'm down."

The tension of the rope eased then, and Sherri hurriedly dug out the skier and turned him over while she waited for Barrett to send down the first-aid kit and the extra harness. She couldn't find the young man's pulse but that might have been because her fingers were chilled and numb from her old injuries. Still, his face was white with cold, not blue with suffocation. That was encouraging. And low temperatures sometimes sent the body into a state almost akin to hibernation. Sherri knew of several instances where people with no pulse had later been warmed to full recovery. She thought she could see the man's chest faintly rising and falling.

A strange noise interrupted her examination. It sounded like a groaning shuffle, and she raised her head. At the same instant Barrett shouted, "Sherri, stand up and free your line!" The terror in his voice was a living thing.

"Not yet," Sherri screamed back, her voice echoing. *Not yet, Barrett,* she pleaded silently. She knew she had only seconds, but seconds were all she needed.

She grabbed the skier around the waist, noting thankfully that the rope was still slack. *Bless you, Barrett,* she thought as she hauled with all her strength and brought them both to a standing position. She immediately tightened her arms around the skier until they ached with the strain and then yelled, "Pull, Barrett, now!"

She didn't think she had finished saying his name before she was flying through the heavy weight of a black, cold dampness. She tightened her arms even more, her fingers locked rigidly around her wrists in a frantic grasp. She had to hold on, but she couldn't for much longer, and she couldn't breathe, either.

"Barrett!" she screamed silently inside her head. "Don't leave me!"

That was the last she remembered. When she opened her eyes, her head was throbbing, her vision foggy, but Barrett's face was just above hers, and she was alive. Alive!

Barrett saw her eyes flutter open, and he wrapped her ever more tightly in his arms. Sherri sighed her relief. They were in the tent Barrett had erected; the skier lay behind them in a sleeping bag.

Sherri reached up one bare hand to touch his cheeks. They were wet with tears.

"Are you okay?" they both asked at the same time.

Sherri smiled. "You have four eyes," she said fuzzily, and Barrett frowned.

"You hit your head on the granite after I pulled you up. I'm afraid I couldn't be too careful with the horse going at a dead run." He held up some fingers. "How many do you see?"

Sherri peered at them in confusion. "Too many for one hand," she complained, then she looked over at the skier. "Is he...?"

"Alive, thanks to you, you little idiot. Can you sit up?"

She could, with his help. "Actually, I don't feel too bad," she said after a couple of minutes, rubbing a growing lump on her head. "Next time I'll have to remember to wear a helmet."

"Are you sure you're okay?" Barrett asked with concern. "The snowstorm is over, and the wind has died down. There's a chopper on the way over right now. You can evacuate with it, you know."

"And leave you all alone in this wilderness? I'd just have to come back for another rescue," she tenderly joked.

Barrett drew her back against his chest, and the two of them sat in peaceful silence until the radio crackled on. Barrett reluctantly picked up the receiver. It was Holden.

"Barrett, the chopper should be reaching your location in a few minutes. Please fire your flares. What is the condition of your patient?"

"He's holding on." Barrett refused to call him "sir."

"And Landers?"

"Is this an official inquiry? Because she's off duty right now, remember?" came the sarcastic answer.

Barrett could certainly hold a grudge, as she knew from personal experience. Sherri reached for the microphone and gently pulled it away from him.

"This is Landers, sir," she said. "Aside from a headache, I'm doing just fine."

"Glad to hear it. Congratulations on the rescue. And I want you to know that I've restored you to full-duty status," he announced, to Sherri's joy. "I could use an assistant chief ranger. Perhaps you'd like to take the job?" he offered. "You're good, Landers, one of the best I've ever seen."

Barrett stiffened, the green eyes suddenly dull as he turned away from her. Sherri knew he'd never stand in the way of her promotion. But a promotion meant working with Holden as a partner, not Barrett. And life without Barrett was something she refused to consider.

She depressed the microphone key. "Thank you, sir, that means a lot to me. But I'm really more valuable out in the field," she said with no hesitation.

"Yes, I suppose you are. Well, I'm sure you'll continue to give me your professional advice. Let me assure you it's always welcome. And the offer to be my assistant stands. You can take me up on it whenever you choose."

Sherri smiled warmly, appreciating his words of professional praise. "Thank you, sir."

"Anytime, Landers, anytime. One more thing. There's been a major snowslide between you and the ranger station. It will take at least two to three days before the avalanche area is safe for travel, and we have another storm predicted before then. You might think about evacuating with the chopper."

Barrett looked at Sherri questioningly. She shook her head knowing that Barrett would understand. There were the horses to consider, for one thing. Besides, her head was already feeling better and her vision was back to normal; she knew the injury wasn't serious.

"We'll stay out in the field," she transmitted.

"Will you have a safe place to wait out the next storm?" Holden asked.

Sherri thought of her father's cabin nestled securely in it familiar hollow. "We know just the place," she responded, and by the satisfied look on Barrett's face, she was aware that he followed her train of thought.

"We'll go light those flares, now," Sherri said. "This i Landers, over and out."

The next half hour was a busy one. The helicopter was unable to land in the deep snow; it could only hover, and the unconscious skier had to be basket-lifted out. Barrett had to take care of that himself, while Sherri stayed with the horses. The animals were frantic, terrified by the noise of the whirling blades, and Sherri was afraid they'd break free and bolt, leaving her and Barrett stranded. Finally the helicopter had gone the rescue equipment and the tent were repacked, and once again, there was just the silence of the mountains around them.

They walked hand-in-hand through the open expanse of snow. The horses were quiet, eyes closed in well-deserved rest as Barrett and Sherri approached.

"I should never have let you go," he said to her, his words crystal clear in the high mountain air.

"I've missed you so much," she gently rebuked, her gloved hand tightening within his.

"I don't suppose you'd be interested in taking me back as your partner, would you?" he asked, emboldened by Sherri's loving expression.

"Only if it's to be a permanent arrangement," she warned.

"Just you try and make it anything else," he said fiercely.

Sherri smiled with contentment. She leaned her head on his shoulder as he let go of her hand to encircle her waist. "Welcome back, partner."

They reached the horses and reluctantly parted to check that the gear and tack were secure for the long ride ahead.

"Why, it's almost dawn," Barrett said in surprise. "The night's over."

"No rest for the weary," Sherri replied, but she wasn't really complaining. She was tired, but it was a comfortable kind of tired, like the contentment one felt after a long journey's end. And Barrett was with her. That was what really counted. She lovingly watched him tighten one final strap, happy to see that he left the mare to her, trusting her to handle the preparations by herself.

A dead tree branch weighed down by snow snapped with a sudden loud report, and the sound echoed against the hills. Sherri laughed with pleasure at the gelding's antics as he kicked and reared at the sudden noise. Barrett's laughter joined hers, and then they were in each other's arms, watching the sun slowly warm the sky with its first morning rays.

# CHAPTER TEN

THE LIGHT FROM THE FIRE shone through Sherri's closed eye lids, and she softly moaned her displeasure. After the helicopter had left with the skier, she and Barrett had ridden all day to reach her cabin. Both had fallen into a dead sleep as soon as the horses had been tended to and the woodpile replenished.

"What time is it?" Sherri asked as she half rose in alarm at the empty space beside her in the bed.

"It's almost three in the morning." Barrett's deep voice filled the cabin. He was wearing only his pants and an unbuttoned shirt.

"My first night's sleep in two days and you wake me up," Sherri protested groggily. "Barrett, come back to bed."

"I will, my love, but after all we've been through, it would be too ironic for us to freeze to death now, especially with a roof over our heads. Let me put some wood on the fire, Sherri. I won't be long."

Sherri sank back into the bed and burrowed deep in the double sleeping bag. It was cool under the covers, but it wouldn't be as soon as Barrett lay beside her again. She watched with loving eyes as he piled on more logs, then quickly stripped and rejoined her in her father's old bed.

"Your feet are like ice!" Sherri gasped as he snuggled against her naked body. "You should have worn your socks," she chided.

"Maybe," he agreed.

The fire made enchanting patterns on the walls, and despite her weariness Sherri was reluctant to close her eyes. "I wonder how long this new storm will last."

"If we're lucky, a good long time." Barrett pulled her close, and the two of them lay side by side, his broad arm holding her a willing prisoner. "This is better than any honeymoon in Seattle," he said contentedly.

"We haven't done anything," Sherri laughed.

"I intend to take care of that," he promised with a glance toward her that sent shivers of delight down her skin.

"We aren't even married yet," she said.

"That didn't stop us before," he reminded her boldly, enjoying her blush. "Besides, I intend to take care of that, too." He laid his cheek against her hair.

"In Portland?" Sherri asked. She didn't wait for him to propose to her again. They understood each other too well to need that formality.

She could feel Barrett shaking his head. "No. My family can fly out here if they want. This is my home now. Colorado's not so bad when *you* come with it."

"True," Sherri agreed shamelessly.

"You have an awfully high opinion of yourself," he scolded, his voice tender. "But rightfully deserved," he added as he planted a firm kiss on her forehead.

Sherri preened at the compliment. "Holden thinks so, too."

At that Barrett sobered. "You do realize you passed up a fantastic promotion. I wouldn't want to stand in the way of your advancement," he said seriously.

Sherri rose on one elbow to look into his face. "If you think you can get rid of your partner that easily, you're dead wrong, Miles Barrett," she retorted. "Pushing papers at some desk isn't my idea of a fun time. Is that…is that what you want for me?" she asked anxiously, afraid he might have ulterior motives for wanting her to take the job as Holden's assistant.

She couldn't help remembering the earlier suffering that Barrett's overprotective attitude had caused her, and she clutched his arm tensely while she waited for his answer.

"It's all right, Sherri. I intend to be your husband, not your jailer," he whispered. His gentle hands and soothing touch gave conviction to his words. "And I'll never, ever make your decisions for you again," he solemnly vowed.

Sherri raised her head. "Even if I ask you to let me risk my life? Even if my job has to come first at times?"

"Even if you ask me to let you stand under a mass of falling snow to help some half-dead stranger," he said with a shudder, his eyes glazing at the memory of the fear he had suffered then. "Only please don't make a habit of it," he pleaded. "My heart can't take it." He drew in a deep breath. "You have my word," he promised with such finality that all Sherri's doubts were put to rest.

"Thank you." She hugged him close, knowing how much that promise had cost him.

Now it was her turn to give comfort, and she dropped light butterfly kisses on his face until the sick fear that filled his eyes had ebbed and died away.

"Besides, I don't intend to do this forever," Sherri assured him. "Maybe in a couple of years we'll be ready for children. When that time comes I'll give up working remote assignments. I intend to put our children to bed myself. I have no intention of leaving it to some stranger."

Barrett ran a hand over her flat stomach with wonder, as if he could already imagine a child of theirs blossoming there.

"And then what? Would you go into administrative duties with Holden?"

"No," Sherri said decisively. "I'd be bored to tears. What I'd really like to do is teach. They're always looking for someone to instruct the new rangers in search and rescue. I'd be perfect for the job."

Barrett's hand slid to her waist to pull her closer. "Well, Landers, since you seem to have everything all mapped out, would you mind telling me when we're planning to create these future little Barretts?"

Sherri's lips curved saucily. "When I've tamed you," she announced.

Barrett laughed heartily, his eyes tearing with mirth. "Then, Sherri, you can expect to have one hell of a long wait," he finally managed to gasp.

Sherri's heart softened at his statement. "I may have to make allowances for you," she amended as she caressed his cheek with the scarred back of one small hand. "Besides, that desk job with Holden would be too time consuming. We'll have our hands full just getting used to being husband and wife," she said, knowing that their personalities were bound to clash despite their love.

Barrett laughed again, but this time his voice was low and husky. "Oh, that won't be too difficult at all," he assured her. "How's your headache?" His eyes burned with a heat that had nothing to do with the room's roaring fire.

"What headache?" Sherri whispered back, her weariness suddenly disappearing as a delicious excitement filled her body.

Barrett lowered his head to her lips, and the two of them met in loving union. His kisses worshipped, adored and then urged her to join him in sweet, primitive surrender. She gave herself with no reservations, and his own loving abandon spoke of perfect trust. The intensity of their passion was so overwhelming that Sherri thought she would die from the sheer pleasure of it. But Barrett was there to bring her gently back, and she knew with certainty in her heart that he would always be there for her.

After one last kiss, she released her passionate hold on Barrett and fell back among the covers. Blissfully she relaxed in his arms, bringing her hand up to tenderly smooth back his disheveled hair.

The firelight caught the gold of Sherri's bracelet, and it glimmered in the dark of the cabin. Barrett gently captured her wrist and brought her palm to his lips.

Sherri smiled with happiness at his action. "I love you, Miles Barrett. Who could have guessed that we'd be anything more than working partners?" She sighed contentedly, her heart finally at peace. "We're such an unlikely combination."

Barrett smiled his superior smile. He urged her even closer, and his eyes gleamed with triumph as her body instantly molded itself to his.

"I wouldn't say that, my love." He felt her tremble anew with rising passion, and his lips moved tantalizingly against hers.

"I wouldn't say that at all."

**Exciting, adventurous, sensual stories of love long ago**

**On Sale Now:**

### SATAN'S ANGEL by Kristin James

*Slater was the law in a land that was as wild and untamed as he was himself, but all that changed when he met Victoria Stafford. She had been raised to be a lady, but that didn't mean she had no will of her own. Their search for her kidnapped cousin brought them together, but they were too much alike for the course of true love to run smooth.*

### PRIVATE TREATY by Kathleen Eagle

*When Jacob Black Hawk rescued schoolteacher Carolina Hammond from a furious thunderstorm, he swept her off her feet in every sense of the word, and she knew that he was the only man who would ever make her feel that way. But society had put barriers between them that only the most powerful and overwhelming love could overcome . . .*

*Look for them wherever Harlequin books are sold.*       HIS-CNM-1

# *Temptation* ™

## TEMPTATION WILL BE
## EVEN HARDER TO RESIST...

In September, Temptation is presenting a sophisticated new
face to the world. A fresh look that truly brings Harlequin's
most intimate romances into focus.

What's more, all-time favorite authors Barbara Delinsky, Rita
Clay Estrada, Jayne Ann Krentz and Vicki Lewis Thompson
will join forces to help us celebrate. The result? A very special
quartet of Temptations...

- **Four striking covers**
- **Four stellar authors**
- **Four sensual love stories**
- **Four variations on one spellbinding theme**

All in one great month! Give in to Temptation in September.

TDESIGN 1

# Coming in April
# *Harlequin Category Romance Specials!*

## Look for six new and exciting titles from this mix of two genres.

### 4 Regencies—lighthearted romances set in England's Regency period (1811-1820)

### 2 Gothics—romance plus suspense, drama and adventure

## Regencies

**Daughters Four** by Dixie Lee McKeone
She set out to matchmake for her sister, but reckoned without the Earl of Beresford's devilish sense of humor.

**Contrary Lovers** by Clarice Peters
A secret marriage contract bound her to the most interfering man she'd ever met!

**Miss Dalrymple's Virtue** by Margaret Westhaven
She needed a wealthy patron—and set out to buy one with the only thing she had of value....

**The Parson's Pleasure** by Patricia Wynn
Fate was cruel, showing her the ideal man, then making it impossible for her to have him....

## Gothics

**Shadow over Bright Star** by Irene M. Pascoe
Did he want her shares to the silver mine, her love—or her life?

**Secret at Orient Point** by Patricia Werner
They seemed destined for tragedy despite the attraction between them....

CAT88A-1